U0165698

應用外語 27

美語口語訓練

第一次用英文接待國外訪客就上手

五南圖書出版公司 印行

ENGLISH

招靜琪　陳彥佑・著

致讀者

　　隨著國際化的來臨，國外來台灣參展，參加研討會的人也愈來愈多。老闆指定讓你去接待嗎？別怕，這本書就是要幫大家學會面對這樣的挑戰，只要盡全力勇敢接待，你就有機會建立長長久久的跨國友誼，不但很有趣，你的努力，也是最實際的國民外交喔！

　　這本書的活動，適合在班級或一群人中使用。如果你自己想鍛鍊口說的功夫，建議你找幾位好朋友一起練習。因為是口說，一定得有人跟你練習才行。當然你也可以儘量假想與人互動的狀況。無論如何，就是要多多開口，確實練習，設想種種情境變化，到時候就能夠把這些說法用出來了。記住喔，你現在不是要參加紙筆測驗，重點是說出口，你的目標是在適當的時機，能夠親口並即時地說出來、用出來！練習的時候，想像情境可以幫上很多忙。

建議練習方式：

- 找個好朋友一起練習，兩人角色扮演，這樣做練習比較不孤單。
- 自己也可以扮演兩個角色，這就不怕說得不好，也不會害羞了。
- 還可以選擇一個錄音角色，然後真人的自己再扮演另一角色（說話的速度要跟上喔）。
- 當然你還可以自行發明其他方法。總而言之，能在練習的同時也覺得好玩是很重要的。

關於訪客接待，有些竅門大家一定要記在心裡。我們台灣人一向最好客了，常常巴不得像7-11一般隨時陪在訪客身邊，亦步亦趨地照顧他們。除非是很害怕新環境的人（這樣的人可能就不會出國了），旅行不就是要四處探險尋找驚奇？為了讓訪客可以好好享受台灣的風土民情，你只要提供足夠的資訊就好。另外，如果別人想學用中文，就不要猛跟他說英文，這感覺好像告訴你的訪客：「我知道你怎麼樣都學不會的啦」，這樣難怪別人不會感激你，反而會有反效果。慢慢去體會，調整好自己的態度與腳步，多蒐集好玩有趣的故事，慢慢設法說給訪客聽，你就會是讓外籍訪客最寬心舒服的異地守護天使、公司裡不可或缺的接待高手喔！

本書一共有七章，20個單元。主要內容以英文呈現，這樣是希望讓你有置身全美語環境中的感覺。但是別擔心，豐富的中文補充內容與翻譯都放在最後的『課文翻譯與解答』中，也歡迎提供改進意見，大家一起為接待外賓努力，讓他們真正享受賓至如歸的感覺！

加油！也希望你真正體驗孔老夫子說的，有朋自遠方來，還真是不亦悅乎啊！

CONTENTS
目錄

Chapter One
Arrival 初來乍到

Unit 1-1 Email Exchange
怎麼寫Email聯絡才不失禮？

01

Email exchange between Professor Green and Oscar

Dear Professor Green,

Thank you for sending me your flight and hotel information. I will personally pick you up at the airport. Please look for the sign with your name on it.

If you would like any special accommodations, please let me know. I will be happy to make arrangements for you.

All of us in the Engineering Department are very excited about your arrival, and we look forward to meeting you in person. Have a pleasant flight!

Regards,
Oscar Lee
Acme, Inc.

 02

Hi Oscar,

Thank you for meeting me at the airport. I really appreciate it. I don't need anything other than stopping by a restaurant for some local food. If it's no trouble, please take me to a traditional breakfast place. I look forward to meeting you and your colleagues.

Regards,
Hank Green
Professor of Mechanical Engineering
University of ABC

1 Listening practice

Professor Green is reading an email from Oscar. Please look through the lines and decide a proper order, and then listen for the actual order on the CD.

 01

Dear Professor Green,

A. I will personally pick you up at the airport.

B. I will be happy to make arrangements for you.

C. Thank you for sending me your flight and hotel information.

D. Have a pleasant flight!

E. If you would like any special accommodations, please let me know.

F. Please look for the sign with your name on it.

G. All of us in the Engineering Department are very excited about your arrival, and we look forward to meeting you in person.

Regards,

Oscar Lee

Acme, Inc.

****

1.____ 2.____ 3.____ 4.____ 5.____ 6.____ 7.____

Oscar is reading an email from Professor Green. Please look through the lines and decide a proper order, and then listen for the actual order.

 02

Hi Oscar:

A. If it's no trouble, please take me to a traditional breakfast place.

B. I really appreciate it.

C. I look forward to meeting you and your colleagues.

D. Thank you for meeting me at the airport.

E. I don't need anything other than stopping by a restaurant for some local food.

Regards,

Hank Green

Professor of Mechanical Engineering

University of ABC

****

1._____ 2._____ 3._____ 4._____ 5._____

Activity 2 Discussion

Discuss the following questions with your classmates.

Both emails above are composed of three parts. What are the three parts? Why are the three parts needed? Please put the three parts in the boxes below.

Activity 3 Understanding and applying words, idioms, and phrases

Part 1

Thank you and Please –

In the two emails above, both of the speakers are very careful with their etiquette. Let us start by learning some simple ways to show our politeness.

Useful expression	Application
1. Thank you for <u>sending</u> me your flight and hotel information. Thank you for <u>the kind gesture.</u>	• Thank you for <u>lunch</u>. • Thank you for <u>picking</u> me up at the hotel. • _____
2. I really appreciate <u>it</u>.	• I really appreciate <u>the dinner.</u> • _____
3. Please <u>look</u> for the sign with your name on it.	• Please <u>have</u> some tea. • _____

Useful expression	Application
4. If you would like <u>any special</u> <u>accommodations</u>, please let me know.	• If you would like <u>any other</u> <u>information</u>, please let me know. • _____
5. If it's no trouble, please <u>take</u> me to a breakfast place that is convenient for you.	• If it's no trouble, please <u>pick me up</u> at the hotel. • _____
6. I don't need anything other than <u>stopping by</u> a traditional breakfast place for some local food.	• I don't need anything other than <u>visiting</u> the 101 Building. • _____
7. I will be happy to <u>make</u> the arrangements.	• I will be happy to <u>bring</u> you some fruits. • _____
8. All of us look forward to <u>meeting</u> you in person.	• We all look forward to <u>your visit</u>. • _____
9. Have a <u>pleasant flight</u>!	• Have a <u>nice weekend</u>! • _____

Part 2

Now we are going to become really familiar with the expressions and use them well. Please pick a number from one to nine. When you get your number, please read out loud the sentence in the box. Then, you will create one statement that is similar to the one that you have just read out loud. Use your facial and voice expressions to gain approval from your teacher and classmates. The student who makes a line first wins the game. Please be polite when you perform.

1

Thank you for sending me your flight and hotel information.

2

I really appreciate it.

3

Please look for the sign with your name on it.

4

If you would like any special accommodations, please let me know.

5

If it's no trouble, please take me to a breakfast place that is convenient for you.

6

I don't need anything other than stopping by a traditional breakfast place for some local food.

7

I will be happy to make the arrangements.

8

All of us look forward to meeting you in person.

9

Have a pleasant flight!

Unit 1-2 Meeting at the Airport

機場接機，訪客會問你什麼問題？

At the airport, Oscar is holding a sign that reads:

03

Prof Green: Hi. (*Extending arm for handshake*). I'm Hank Green. You must be Oscar.

Oscar: Hi, Professor Green. (*Extending arm for handshake*). Yes, I'm Oscar.

Green: Very nice to meet you, Oscar. Thank you for picking me up.

Oscar: It's my pleasure. It looks like you have all your bags. This way please. A car is waiting for us outside the building. How was the flight?

Green: Hmm... It was a little bit bumpy during landing; otherwise, it was a pretty smooth flight. But I couldn't eat on the plane, with the noise and everything... and I am a bit hungry now.

Oscar: OK. Let's get out of here and have some breakfast. How about taking you some place decent?

Green: Thank you, but that's OK. I'll grab a quick bite to eat in the hotel cafe. I'm sure you have plenty of things to finish up before the conference.

Oscar: It's no trouble at all. Plus, I have to eat, too.

Green: In that case, do you mind if we get some Chinese donuts and the flaky sesame pastry?

Oscar: Got it! I know just the place.

Green: Fantastic! Thanks again, Oscar. I'm famished.

Activity 1 Listening practice

Listen to the CD and put the sentences you hear in the blanks.

🎧 04

****

Part 1

Green: Hi. I'm Hank Green. _____

Oscar: Hi, Professor Green. Yes, I am Oscar.

Green: Very nice to meet you, Oscar. _____

Oscar: It's my pleasure.

******

Part 2

Oscar: _____ Let's get out of here and have some breakfast.

_____

Green: Thank you, but that's OK. _____ I'm sure you have plenty of things to finish up before the conference.

Oscar: _____ Plus, I have to eat too.

Green: _____ do you mind if we get some Chinese donuts and the flaky sesame pastry?

Oscar: Got it! _____

Green: _____ Thanks again, Oscar. _____

(A) It's no trouble at all.

(B) I'm famished.

(C) It looks like you have all your bags.

(D) In that case,

(E) Thank you for picking me up.

(F) I know just the place.

(G) How about taking you some place decent?

(H) She is unable to meet you here.

(I) Fantastic!

(J) You must be Oscar.

(K) I'll grab a quick bite in the hotel cafe.

Activity 2 Discussion

Part 1

You just arrived in a country which you have never been. What would you like to know now? What questions would you ask? Discuss with your partner and list three questions here. What would be some possible answers?

1. _____

2. _____

3. _____

Part 2

In the video below a tourist has just arrived at the Taoyuan International Airport. Watch the video and decide what questions the tourist has for the driver and what they are talking about. (Pay attention to their interaction between 0:33 and 2:20 only.) What should the driver say?

Getting out of Taipei Taoyuan Airport (by Networks from A to Z, 2014)

https://www.YouTube.com/watch?v=-Wbv9LfTAXg

If you have figured out the questions already, please see the transcript below and decide what the driver should have said:

- Driver : In Taiwan, one? Two? (**He could say:** _____

  _____?)

- Tourist: First time.

- Driver : Taiwan food? (**He could say:** _____?)

- Tourist: Yes, I think I will try. ... How long to the hotel? 10 minutes? 15 minutes? Two o'clock? One?

- Driver : Yes, two. (**He could say:** _____
        _____?)
- Tourist: Very hot. I like.
- Driver : Hot. Good. (**He could say:** _____.)

Practice and make sure that you can respond to the basic questions that the tourist asks. Be prepared that they will ask you more. What other questions do you think visitors will ask?

Activity 3 Understanding and applying words, idioms, and phrases

Useful expression	Definition	Application
1. pick sb. up	接某人	• My father picks me up at the train station every afternoon. • _____
2. How about ...	…如何（怎麼樣）？（建議用）	• How about we have noodles for lunch? • _____
3. Do you mind if ...?	你介意…嗎？（建議用）	• Do you mind if we take a taxi? • _____
4. It looks like ...	看起來、好像…	• It looks like he could never be on time. • _____
5. I'm sure (that) ...	我很確定…	• I'm sure you will enjoy Taipei. • _____

Useful expression	Definition	Application
6. I'm famished.	我餓扁了	• I am famished. Let's get something to eat first! • _____
7. In that case, ...	這樣的話…	• In that case, let's eat first and then go shopping. • _____
8. It's my pleasure to...	…是我的榮幸	• It's my pleasure to serve you, Ma'am. • _____
9. It's no trouble at all to...	一點都不麻煩	• It's no trouble at all to show you around. I am free all day. • _____
10.I'll grab a quick bite.	我就隨便吃吃	• I'll grab a quick bite on the way to the airport. • _____

More useful expressions

1. 飛機晚了 My flight was late.
   飛機早到了 My flight arrived early.
   飛機準時到達 My flight arrived on time.
2. 機場 airport
   入境 arrival
   離境 departure
   轉乘 transfer
   領取行李 luggage claim

1-3 **Telling Directions** 如何告知搭車選項？

Ms. Tan just exited customs and immigration at Taoyuan International Airport and is asking for directions from Ray and his mother.

🎧05

Ms. Tan:	Excuse me, Sir. Do you speak some English?
Ray:	Um, yes.
Ms. Tan:	Oh, good! Can you please help me with directions?
Ray:	Sure, I think so.
Ms. Tan:	I'd like to go to Taipei Main Station from here. Unfortunately, there's a mix up with my driver and I can't reach my contact person.
Ray:	OK. I think you can take a taxi. I can talk to the driver for you. It's the easiest way.

Ms. Tan: Um, I was thinking about riding the shuttle bus because I'm not so comfortable with taking a taxi by myself.

Ray: I see what you mean. How about taking the express bus?

Ms. Tan: That could work. Once I reach Taipei Main Station, I know how to take the MRT so I should be able to find my hotel. It's not my first time in Taipei.

Ray: I can help you buy a bus ticket, but we have to wait a little bit for my mother to exit customs. Oh hey. There she is. (*Ray's mom approaches.*)

Ray's mom: Hi!

(*Ray and his mom have a short conversation in Mandarin.*)

Ray: My mom says you should ride with us. We can take you to your hotel since we are going back to Taipei anyway.

Ms. Tan: Oh no, no. Thank you so much. I shouldn't trouble you. Please tell her that.

(*Ray and his mom have another short conversation in Mandarin.*)

Ray: She asks if you are sure. It's no trouble for us.
             And... she asked where you are from.

Ms. Tan: That's very sweet of her. But I can manage on my own. And, I'm from Australia. My parents are from Singapore.

(*Another quick conversation between mother and son.*)

Ray: OK, then. If that's the case, let me help you get on the right bus.

Ms. Tan: I appreciate that. Thank you so much. (*To Ray's mom*): Hsieh hsieh ni.

Ray's mom: You're welcome.

Activity 1 Listening practice

 05

Circle the words or pictures that correspond with the conversation.

Ms Tan: Excuse me, sir. Do you speak some ● / ⌗ ?

Ray: Um, yes.

Ms. Tan: Oh, good! Can you please help me with (directions / detections)?

Ray: Sure. I think so.

Ms. Tan: I'd like to go to from here. Unfortunately, there's a mix up with my driver and I can't reach my (contact / connect) person.

Ray: OK. I think you can take a . I can talk to the driver for you. It's the easiest way.

Ms. Tan: Um, I was thinking about riding the (shuttle / shuffle) bus because I'm not so comfortable with taking a taxi by myself.

Ray: I see what you mean. How about taking the express?

Ms. Tan: That could work. Once I reach Taipei Main Station, I know

how to take the 🚛 / 🚃 so I should be able to find my

🏠 / 🍷 . It's not my first time in Taipei.

Ray: I can help you buy a bus ticket, but we have to wait a little bit for my mother to exit (customs / cartoons). Oh hey. There she is.

(*Ray's mom approaches.*)

Ray's mom: Hi!

(*Ray and his mom have a short conversation in Mandarin.*)

Ray: My mom says you should (ride / type) with us. We can take you to your hotel since we are going back to Taipei (anyway / everywhere).

Ms. Tan: Oh no, no. Thank you so much. I shouldn't (trouble / bother) you. Please tell her that.

(*Ray and his mom have another short conversation in Mandarin.*)

Ray: She asks if you are sure. It's no trouble for us. And... she asked where you are from.

Ms. Tan: That's very sweet of her. But I can (maintain / manage) on my own. And, I'm from Australia. My parents are from (Singapore / Switzerland).

(*Another quick conversation between mother and son.*)

Ray: OK, then. If that's the case, let me help you get (on / in) the right bus.

Ms. Tan: I (accustom / appreciate) that. Thank you so much.

(*To Ray's mom*): Hsieh hsieh ni.

Ray's mom: You're welcome.

Activity 2 Discussion

1. Why does Ms. Tan reject Ray's mother's invitation of taking a ride with them? Is it the same reason that makes her uncomfortable to take a taxi?

2. In the conversation, how many options are there for Ms. Tan to get to Taipei Main Station? How many options can you think of if you are to go from the airport to a well-known hotel in your city? Please tell the options to your friend.

Activity 3 Understanding and applying words, idioms, and phrases

Part 1

Understand the meaning of the expressions and try to create new sentences or short dialogues with them. Make sure you know the Chinese meaning of the following expressions.

Useful expression	Application
1. Can you please help me with...?	• Can you please help me with this heavy box? • _____
2. There's a mix-up ...	• There's a mix-up in the schedule. • _____
3. I was thinking about V-ing	• I was thinking about getting married. • _____
4. I'm not so comfortable with Sth / V-ing	• I'm not so comfortable with a stranger. • _____
5. Once S+V, S+V	• Once you know him, you will like him. • _____
6. ... on one's own	• I can fill in the tax return on my own. • _____
7. If that's the case, ...	• A: It's an old car, as old as your father. B: If that's the case, I'll never ask for it. • _____
8. It's no trouble for us.	• We'd love to do that for you. It's no trouble for us. • _____

Useful expression	Application
9. That's very sweet of her.	• A: Sally said that she could be your helper in the Toastmasters. B: That's very sweet of her. • _____
10.1 appreciate that.	• A: We will take you to the airport. B: I appreciate that. • _____

Part 2

Form a group of 3~4. Each group member needs to write down his/her home address in English. Tell one another how you go to school and what kind of transportation you take. Each one should use as many of the above expressions as they can. Use your smartphone to check your English address on the following website 郵局中文地址英譯http://www. post.gov.tw/post/internet/Postal/index.jsp?ID=207

(If privacy is a concern, you may create an address to use in this activity.)

Example:

Your Turn:

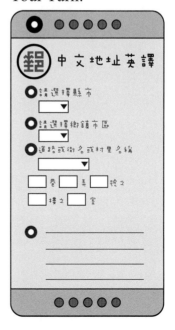

Example: Jessie's Story

Group Members	Home address	Transportation	Time for transportation
Jessie	No. 1, Chung-Hwa Rd., Taichung	by bus and on foot	Around 45 minutes

My name is Jessie. I live at No. 1, Chung-Hwa Rd., Taichung. It's no trouble for me to go from home to school because there are some bus stops near my house. Usually I take a bus to school. After getting off the bus, I need to take a 10-minute walk to get to school. Sometimes, if the weather is bad, my mom would drive me to school. I really appreciate that.

Chapter Two
Making Yourself at Home 賓至如歸

Unit 2-1 Solving Problems with the Network
幫忙解決網路問題

This unit begins with Professor Green reading an instruction card for connecting to the hotel wireless network.

06

Dear Valued Guests,

Hotel Oceanside is pleased to provide free WiFi access during your stay with us.

To connect to Hotel Oceanside WiFi:

1. Turn on your wireless card

2. View all wireless networks and select "Hotel-WiFi"

3. Enter password: oceanside

4. Enjoy the free WiFi!

Ethernet cables are available at the front desk.

Thank you. We hope you have a wonderful stay with us.

Regards,

Technical Support Center

Hotel Oceanside

🎧 07

Front Desk: Good evening. How can I help you?

Prof. Green: Hi. I'm having trouble connecting to the hotel wireless network. I followed the instructions on the guest info card but it didn't work.

Front Desk: I'm sorry about that, Sir. Could you hold while I check the availability of our IT specialist?

Prof. Green: Yes, no problem.

Front Desk: Great. Thank you.

...Moments later...

Front Desk: Sir, thanks for holding. Our IT specialist is available now to solve your connection problem. Should I ask him to come to your room in the next 10 minutes?

Prof. Green: Yes. That would be wonderful. Thank you for your help. I really appreciate it.

Front Desk: You're welcome, Sir. I hope you have a pleasant evening.

Prof. Green: Thanks. Same to you.

Activity 1 Listening practice

Please look through the lines and fill in the blanks, and then listen for the correct answers on the CD.

🎧 08

Front Desk: Good afternoon. (1) _____

Prof. Green: Yes. I'm having trouble connecting to the hotel wireless network. (2) _____

Front Desk: (3) _____ Could you hold for a few minutes while I check the availability of our IT specialist?

Prof. Green: Yes, no problem.

Front Desk: Great. Thank you.

... Moments later ...

Front Desk: Sir, (4) _____ Our IT specialist is available now to solve your connection problem. (5) _____

Prof. Green: Yes. (6) _____ Thank you for your help. (7) _____

Front Desk: You're welcome, Sir. (8) _____

Prof. Green: Thank you.

(A) How can I help you?   (B) I hope you have a pleasant stay.
(C) I really appreciate it.   (D) thanks for holding.
(E) Should I ask him to visit your room in five minutes?
(F) That would be wonderful.   (G) I'm sorry about that, Sir.
(H) I followed the instructions on the guest info card but it didn't work.

---

1. ____ 2. ____ 3. ____ 4. ____ 5. ____ 6. ____ 7. ____ 8. ____

Activity 2 Discussion

1. In Taiwan, which public areas can you usually get free WiFi? Please tell your friends in English where and how they can connect a smart phone to free WiFi in your city.
2. Form a group of 3~4. First, think about the Chinese names of the following telecom companies. Second, compare and contrast different telecom companies, focusing particularly on the prices and network service that they offer to short-term international visitors. Which companies are better in which aspects?

Telecom company	Chinese name	Advantages & disadvantages for short-term international visitors
Taiwan Star Telecom		
Asia Pacific Telecom		
Chunghwa Telecom		
VIBO Telecom		
Far EasTone		
Taiwan Mobile		

Activity 3 Understanding and applying words, idioms, and phrases

Part 1
Useful expressions

Useful expression	Definition	Application
1. connecting to	連接到…	• He connected the TV to an outlet. • _____
2. wireless network	無線網路	• Wireless network connections are available all over the city. • _____
3. be pleased to	很高興	• I'm pleased to be your guide. • _____
4. available	（在手邊）可利用的	• The coupon is not available. • _____
5. Hope you have a wonderful stay with us.	希望你在我們旅館住得愉快。（短暫地住叫做stay長住在家中叫做live。）	• Hope you have a wonderful trip. • _____
6. have trouble + Ving	有…麻煩	• We are having trouble naming our baby. • _____

Useful expression	Definition	Application
7. it didn't work	行不通	• The man tried to repaired the TV, but it didn't work. • _____
8. the availability of	有效性,可得到的東西	• Before traveling, we must ensure the availability of gas. • _____
9. Thank you for holding.	謝謝你等候。	• Hold a second. • _____
10. solve your connection problem	解決你的連接問題 Help you with your connection problem	• My son can solve your connection problem immediately. • _____
11. I really appreciate it.	我真的很感激。	• I appreciate your help. • _____
12. Same to you.	你也是一樣。	• A: Congratulations! B: Thank you. Same to you. • _____

Part 2

Below are some commonly-used acronyms and abbreviations. Do you know more?

IT specialist	Information technology	資訊工程人員
E.E. (pronounced as "Double E")	Electronical engineer	電子工程師
CNN (I)		
BBC		
L. A.		

DIY	Do it yourself.	C & P	Copy and paste
LOL	Laughing out loud	2F4Y	Too fast for you
HF	Have fun	RSVP	Repondez s'il vous plait (French: Please reply)
BTW	By the way	NA	Not available
IDK	I don't know.	OMG	
TBA		TYT	

Email exchanges between Professor Green and Oscar on the evening after the professor's arrival in Taipei

 09

Hi Oscar,

I'm sorry for this sudden request. I strained my back just now and am experiencing some discomfort. Would you please advise what medical options are available to me? If possible, please give me an idea about the level of expenses I can expect. I feel that I'm in good hands with your help. Many thanks.

Regards,
Hank Green

10

Dear Professor Green,

I hope you are feeling better by now. Tomorrow, I can take you to the local hospital for an evaluation. Depending on what the doctor says, we also have the option of visiting an acupuncturist or a massage therapist. I am not sure about the costs because with Taiwan's universal health coverage, patients do not pay the full amount. Based on my understanding, however, the cost of a regular visit shouldn't be more than US$30. The cost of an acupuncturist visit should be roughly the same.

If you have any questions, we can discuss it in detail in person.
Best wishes and see you tomorrow.

Regards,
Oscar

 11

Hi, Oscar,

Thank you so much for the quick response. I feel less anxious now that I know what my options are in Taiwan. See you tomorrow.

Regards,
Hank Green

Activity 1 Listening practice

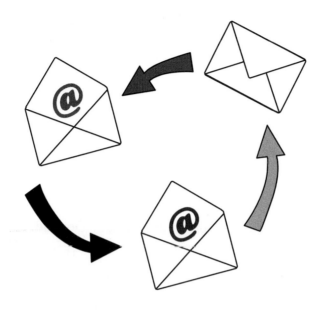

 09

Part 1

Read the following expressions first. Listen to the CD. Put the steps in order based on what you hear.

A. I'm sorry for this sudden request.

B. I feel that I'm in good hands with your help. Many thanks in advance.

C. Would you please advise what medical options are available to me?

D. If possible, please also give me an idea about the level of expenses I can expect.

E. I strained my back just now and am experiencing some discomfort.

1. ____ 2. ____ 3. ____ 4. ____ 5. ____

Part 2

You are going to hear two return emails. First, read the following emails. Then, fill in the blanks based on what you hear.

 10

Dear Professor Green,

I hope you are feeling better by now. Tomorrow, I can take you to the (1)_____ _____ for an evaluation. Depending on what the doctor says, (2)_____ _____ _____ the option of visiting an acupuncturist or a massage therapist. I am not sure about the costs because with Taiwan's universal health coverage, patients do not (3)__ _____ _____ _____ _____ . Based on my understanding, however, the cost of a regular visit shouldn't cost you more than US$30. The cost of an acupuncturist visit should be roughly the same. (4)_____ _____ _____ _____ _____ , we can discuss it in detail in person.

Best wishes and see you tomorrow.

Regards,
Oscar

Hi, Oscar,

Thank you so much (5)_____ _____ _____ _____ . I feel less anxious now that I know what my options are in Taiwan. See you tomorrow.

Regards,
Hank Green

Activity 2 Discussion

1. Discuss with your friends what other medical needs visitors or tourists might have when they travel. How do you say these needs in English and how would you help them?
2. If you hurt your back, who would you see to cure your back, a doctor, an acupuncturist, or a masseuse? Why? Please have a debate with your friends: What is the best way to heal a pulled muscle, see a doctor or an acupuncturist?

Activity 3 Understanding and applying words, idioms, and phrases

Part 1

Check your smart phone for more information about the following useful expressions. Familiarize yourself with the following useful expressions and then make your own sentences.

Useful Expression	Definition	Application
1. strained one's back	扭到	• My grandma_____ when she stood up. • _____
2. option	選擇	• It's your option to buy or to rent. • How many _____ do I have?
3. If possible, ...	假如可能的話…	• If possible, I'll visit your family. • _____
4. in good hands	妥善得到照顧	• My mom is glad to know that her money is in good hands. • _____
5. in advance	事先	• I need to book train tickets in advance during New Year. • Our teacher had us_____in advance.
6. Depending on ...	依靠…	• Depending on how you feel, choose one of the options. • _____
7. Based on ...	以…為基礎 / 基於	• Based on my knowledge, she is quite popular among young people. • _____
8. roughly the same	大約一樣	• My twin brother's and my scores are roughly the same. • _____

Useful Expression	Definition	Application
9. in detail	詳細說明	• Your report should be explained in detail. • _____
10. in person	親自 / 本人	• I'll see her in person. • _____

*acupuncturis 針灸醫生   *massage therapist 按摩師

*National Health Insurance 全民健保

 12

Part 2

While playing the CD, please listen carefully to an email that is composed with the language provided above. Then, give a summary of the story in your own words and identify which of the above expressions are included in the story. You may need to play it twice to get the summary right.

★☆★ Main idea:

_____

How many expressions and patterns have you heard? _____

Part 3

The story above uses many of the expressions that we have learned. How many of the expressions can you use to form one or many sentences? For this activity, you need to use two of the twelve expressions below to create a sentence in thirty seconds. Let's see who can create accurate and fun sentences. Practice as often as you can until you are quick and correct.

1. roughly	2. opion	3. in detail
4. strain my back	5. massage therapist	6. in person
7. If possible, ...	8. in good hands	9. in advance
10. available	11.the same	12. Based on ...

Unit 2-3 Enjoying the City on Your Own
讓他自由自在趴趴走

Grant is from the US, visiting Taipei for a trade show. He is talking with his colleague, Ray, from the Taipei branch office. They are friends so their word choices are informal.

13

Grant: Hey, Ray. Do you have a minute?

Ray: Sure. What's up?

Grant: As you know, attending the trade show is my main objective in Taipei. However, I'd also like to visit a few of the retail displays that are in the department stores.

Ray: Ah, that's a great idea. I can take you anytime you'd like.

Grant: Thanks for the offer. I want to ask you for directions to Miramar (美麗華) and take a look at our counter there.

Ray: You mean the shopping center with the giant ferries wheel, right? It's easy to get there, but I really don't mind taking you this weekend.

Grant: No, man. You should spend the weekend with your family. Besides, I can explore the city by myself tomorrow. It'll be fun.

Ray: In that case, let me write up the directions for you. Give me a couple of minutes.

Grant: Sounds good. Thanks a lot.

Ray: You're welcome. It's a piece of cake.

Activity 1 Listening practice

 13

Listen to the CD and fill in the blanks with the correct letter.

Grant:	Hey Ray. Do you_____?
Ray:	Sure._____?
Grant:	As you know, attending the trade show is my_____in Taipei. However, I'd also like to visit a few of the_____ that are in the department stores.
Ray:	Ah, that's a great idea. I can take you_____.
Grant:	_____. I want to ask you for directions to Miramar. We have a counter there.
	....
Ray:	You mean the shopping center with the giant_____, right? It's easy to get there, but I _____ taking you this weekend.
Grant:	_____. You should spend the weekend with your family. Besides, I can_____by myself tomorrow. _____.
Ray:	In that case, let me_____the directions for you. Give me_____.
Grant:	Sounds good. Thanks a lot.
Ray:	You're welcome. _____.

(A) have a minute
(B) anytime you 'd like
(C) retail displays
(D) Thanks for the offer
(E) main objective
(F) What 's up
(G) explore the city
(H) No, man
(I) write up
(J) ferris wheel
(K) a couple of minutes
(L) It 's a piece of cake.
(M) really don 't mind
(N) It 'll be fun

Activity 2 Discussion

Part 1

1. What informal words do Grant and Ray use which show their friendship?
2. If you were Grant, would you like Ray to take you or to explore the city by yourself? Why?
3. Actually many international visitors enjoy exploring the city on their own, but as a friend to them, what do you think tourists will need in order to enjoy the city and be safe? What advice would you give them to help them enjoy the city and be safe?

Part 2

Act out the dialogue with a partner. The dialogue could be similar, but remember to change the reasons you choose to accept or reject Ray's offer. Ray could also offer some useful advice to Grant.

Activity 3 Understanding and applying words, idioms, and phrases

Part 1

Check the Chinese meaning of the phrases or sentences below and discuss with a partner in what situations are these phrases and sentences often used. Then, use some expressions to create interesting short dialogues.

1. Do you have a minute?
2. What 's up?
3. Thanks for the offer.
4. You mean ...
5. I really don 't mind taking you this weekend.

6. No, man.

7. Let me write up the direction for you.

8. In that case, ...

9. Give me a couple of minutes.

10. Sounds good.

11. It 's a piece of cake.

 14

Example:

Hi, Luke. <u>Do you have a minute?</u>

Sure thing. <u>What's up?</u>

Would you like to go to my birthday party? The girl you have a crush on will be there.

<u>Hey, man.</u> Why didn't you tell me earlier? Sure, I will be there.

Part 2

Pair work. Fill in the blanks using the above expressions while practicing the following dialogues.

(A)

Sorry, Nancy, I can't attend the meeting around 9 because I need to drop off some papers at Sogo University around 10.

_____, let's change the time. How about 10:30?

That'll be great!

(B)

Hi, Johnny. Do you have a minute?

Sure. _____

I'll buy a motorbike. Are you free to go with me this afternoon?

Cool! I'd love to.

_____.

You're very welcome.

Chapter Three
Arriving at the Conference 會場報到

Unit 3-1 Checking in at the Conference
會場報到會說什麼？

Dennis: Hello. Welcome to the conference. May I have your name, please?

Davis: Hi. Yes, my name is Jane Davis.

Dennis: Just a moment, please. Let me take a look. Ah, here it is. It's nice to meet you, Professor Davis. Here is your badge and your meal voucher.

Davis: Thank you. I requested a vegetarian meal so can you please verify that for me?

Dennis: Certainly. This voucher is green, which means that you will be provided a vegetarian lunch and beverage.

Davis: Great.

Dennis: Also, here's a complimentary tote bag that contains a conference agenda, a floor plan, as well as some promotional items from our sponsors.

Davis: Wonderful. This is exactly what I need.

           Just a very quick question: Where and when is the next keynote speech?

Dennis: The next keynote speech starts in about five minutes in the main hall, which is next to the elevator on your right.

Davis: Oh, good. I have a few more minutes.

Dennis: If you have any questions or need any help, all of us are here to assist.

Davis: Fantastic. I noticed that the staff are wearing bright colored vests.

Dennis: Yes, hard to miss. We are very bright.

Davis: Indeed. Thank you very much for your help.

Dennis: You're welcome, Professor Davis. Have a good time.

Activity 1 Listening practice

Listen to the CD and circle the word you hear.

🎧 17

Dennis: Hello. Welcome to the conference. May I have your (name / phone number / age), please?

Davis: Hi. Yes, my name is Jane Davis.

Dennis: Just a (minute / moment / second), please. Let me take a look. Ah, here it is.

It's nice to have you Professor Davis. Here is your name (back / pack / badge) and your meal voucher.

Davis: Thank you. I (stayed / requested / asked) for a vegetarian meal so can you please (verify / vary /carry) that for me?

Dennis: Certainly. This voucher is (green / free / tree), which means that you will be provided a vegetarian lunch and (soda / beverage / drink).

Davis: Great.

Dennis: Also, here's a complimentary tote bag that contains a conference agenda, a floor plan, as well as some (promotional items / additional ideas) from our sponsors.

Davis: Wonderful. This is exactly what I need.

Just a very (clear / quick / small) question: where and when is the next keynote speech?

Dennis: The next keynote speech starts (at / on / in) about five minutes in the main hall, which is next to the elevator on your (ride / right / side).

Davis: Oh, good. I have a few more minutes.

Dennis: If you have any (station / problems / questions) or need any help, all of us are here to assist.

Davis: Fantastic. I noticed that the staff members are wearing (bright / tight / white) colored vests.

Dennis: Yes, hard to (cross / miss / pass). We are very bright.

Davis: Indeed. Thank you very much for your help.

Dennis: You're welcome, Professor Davis. Have a good time.

Activity 2 Discussion

1. Have you ever attended any conferences or meetings? What was the conference or meeting about? Talk about this experience.
2. What information do you think will appear on the name badge?
3. When was the last time you checked in? Where did you check in? Was it at a hotel, at a conference, or at an airport?

Activity 3 Understanding and applying words, idioms, and phrases

Part 1

In this conversation, you see many objects that are used in conferences, such as the badge and meal voucher. Let's learn what these objects look like and how you use them.

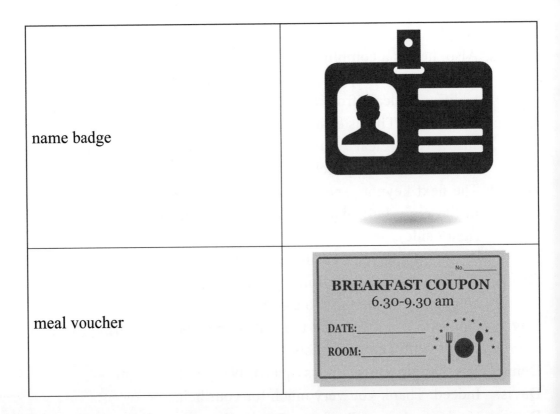

| name badge | |
| meal voucher | |

vegetarian meal	
complimentary tote bag	
conference agenda	
floor plan	
promotional items	

keynote speech

Part 2

In addition to the objects, Denise as the receptionist also uses some expressions that are formal and polite. When you want to show respect, make sure that you know how to use the following expressions.

➢ May I have your name, please?

➢ Just a moment, please.

➢ Here is your ...

➢ If you have any questions or need any help, all of us are here to assist.

➢ Have a good time.

Part 3

Drama time

Please work in pairs to create a three-minute dialogue. You must use three of the objects or expressions from this unit. Practice well for five to ten minutes and then perform on the stage.

Unit 3-2 Responding to Requests
如何回應相關需求？

🎧18

Grant: Excuse me. I don't have a list of keynote speakers in my conference attendee's package. Do you have additional copies?

Staff 1:   I'm sorry. Could you please say that again?

Grant: Sure, of course. Could you please give me a copy of the list of keynote speakers? It's not in this complimentary tote bag.

Staff 1:   Ah, okay. I understand. (*Hands Grant another tote bag containing all the conference information.*)

Grant: Oh, no, I don't need another bag. I only need a list of the speakers.

Staff 1:   Um ... Sorry, please wait a moment.

Grant: Okay. Take your time.

Staff 2:   Hi. How can I help you?

Grant: Hello. Yes. I didn't receive a copy of the list of keynote speakers. Do you have an extra copy for me?

Staff 2: Ah, yes of course. Sorry for any confusion. Let me get one right now.

Grant: It's okay. Don't apologize. Thank you both very much.

Activity 1 Listening practice

Part 1

Listen to the CD and fill the blanks with proper answers.

 18

(A) a list of keynote speakers   (B) apologize   (C)a copy of   (D) wait a moment   (E) extra   (F) any confusion   (G) complimentary tote bag   (H) take your time

Grant: Excuse me. Hi. I don't have (1) _____in my conference attendee's package. Do you have additional copies?

Staff 1: I'm sorry. Can you please say that again?

Grant: Sure, of course. Can you give me (2) _____ the list of keynote speakers? It's not in this (3) _____.

Staff 1: Ah, okay. I understand.
(*Hands Grant another tote bag containing all the conference information.*)

Grant: Oh no. I don't need another bag. I only need a list of the speakers.

Staff 1: Um ... Sorry, please (4) _____.

Grant: Okay. (5) _____.

Staff 2: Hi. How can I help you?

Grant: Hello. Yes. I didn't receive a copy of the list of keynote speakers. Do you have an (6) _____copy for me?

Staff 3: Ah, yes of course. Sorry for (7) _____. Let me get one right now.

Grant: It's okay. Don't (8) _____. Thank you both very much.

Part 2

Listen to the CD again and choose the correct answer for each question.

 19

Question 1:
(A) A name tag.
(B) A list of speakers.
(C) A timetable.
(D) A bag.

Question 2:
(A) A book.
(B) A piece of paper.
(C) A bag.
(D) A list.

Activity 2 Discussion

1. Have you ever been asked a question unexpectedly by an international visitor? Tell your friends about such an experience and how you felt.
2. In a globalized community today, there will be many unexpected opportunities that require you to use English. Please discuss what strategies you can use to increase your ability to respond to unexpected English questions.
3. On the other hand, many of the international visitors in Taiwan are here to learn Chinese. How do you think they would feel if we insist on speaking English to them? Would it be possible that they feel

unwelcomed or unappreciated? Why?

4. If you know that an international visitor is here to learn Chinese and if they do not understand your Chinese, what are some ways to help them understand more using only Chinese, not English?

Activity 3 Understanding and applying words, idioms, and phrases

Part 1

Learn some useful expressions. Check your smartphone and fill in the following blanks on your own.

Useful expression	Definition	Application
1. a list of		
2. keynote speaker		
3. attendee		
4. a copy of		
5. contain		
6. apologize		

Part 2

If you can learn to use the statements below, you will be considered a polite young person. Please discuss with your friends when you will need these statements.

1. Can you please say that again?
2. Please wait a moment.
3. Take your time.
4. How can I help you?
5. Sorry for any confusion.
6. Don't apologize.

Part 3

Work in pairs. Together please carefully study the dialogues below. Choose among the six statements in Part 2 to fill in the blanks. Then, pick one of the dialogues and extend it to create and perform a one-minute skit for the class.

Question 1:

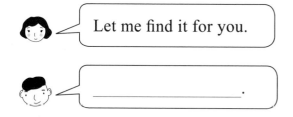

Let me find it for you.

_____.

Question 2:

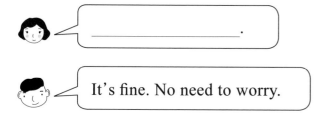

_____.

It's fine. No need to worry.

Question 3:

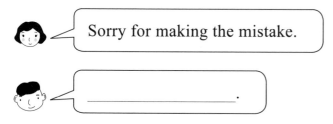

Sorry for making the mistake.

_____.

Question 4:

_____.

Oh, I have some problem with the computer.

Question 5:

I want a cup of tea, please.

I can't hear you. _____.

Question 6:

Is your boss here? I would like to see him.

Sure. _____.

Chapter Four
Attending the Conference 參加會議

Unit 4-1 **Welcoming Remarks**
如何代表大會致歡迎詞？

In the conference hall, Sarah is holding the microphone and speaking to the audience.

20

Dear Colleagues,

Good morning! It's really wonderful to see everyone here. Let me welcome you to the first day of our annual meeting. My name is Sarah Yang, VP of marketing and sales.

We have an exciting day ahead of us, but before we begin, I'd like to remind everyone to please switch your mobile phones to silent mode. Thank you.

In your hands, you should have the agenda for today. For the majority of the morning, our CEO, a special guest and I will lead you through Acme's marketing goals for the next fiscal year. After lunch, you will join your team for group meetings. We will end this day with happy hour in our employee lounge.

Our staff has done a great job organizing this conference. We hope you will find it a fulfilling and enjoyable experience. With that, please welcome our CEO, Mr. Morgan Lee.

Conference Agenda

Day One		Presenter
09:00-09:15	Welcome and Intro	Sarah Yang (Vice President of Marketing/ Sales, Acme, Inc.)
09:15-10:15	Keynote Presentation	Morgan Lee (CEO, Acme, Inc.) Hank Green (Professor, University of ABC)
10:15-10:30	Break	
10:30-12:00	Keynote Presentation Continued Q&A	
12:00-1:30	Lunch	
1:30-3:00	Business Unit Group Meetings	
3:00-5:00	Happy Hour	

Activity 1 Listening practice

20

Part 1

Listen carefully to the CD and circle the words you hear.

Sarah (speaking):

Dear Colleagues, good morning! It's really (wonderful / beautiful) to see everyone. Here, let me welcome you to the first day of our (monthly / annual) meeting. My name is Sarah Yang, VP (Vice President) of marketing and sales.

We have an exciting day (ahead of / in front of) us, but before we begin, I'd like to (tell / remind) everyone to please switch your mobile phones to silent-mode. Thank you.

In your hands, you should have the (agenda / activity) for today. For the majority of the morning, our CEO, a special guest and I will lead you through Acme's marketing goals for the next fiscal year. After lunch, you will join your team for (group meetings / tea break). We will end this day with a happy hour in our employee lounge.

Our staff has done a great job organizing this conference. We hope you will find it (an interesting / a fulfilling) and enjoyable experience. With that, please welcome our CEO, Mr. Morgan Lee.

Part 2

Listen to the CD carefully and answer the questions. You will listen to the CD twice.

Question 1:   What do you need to do before the meeting?

A.   B.   C.   D.

22

Question 2:   Who is the most likely person you will see after this announcement?

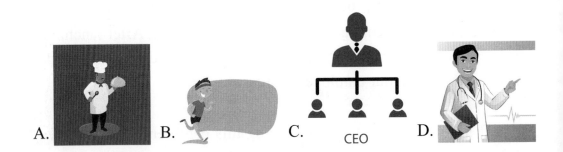

A.   B.   C.   CEO   D.

Activity 2 Discussion

1. Analyze the structure of Sarah's talk. What did she say to start? What information is included? How did she end? What is the purpose of this brief talk? Then, you need to create a similar talk for an event of your choice. Practice and present it in front of the class.

2. When was the last time you thought a cell phone rang at a wrong

time? Was the phone yours? How did you feel when the phone rang at a wrong time? Discuss this experience with your friends.

Activity 3 Understanding and applying words, idioms, and phrases

Part 1

Besides silent mode, what other modes does a cell phone have? Take out your smartphone and compare it with your partner's. Do you have the following modes? Discuss with your friends when or where each of these modes is used.

FLIGHT/ AIRPLANE MODE	NORMAL MODE	OUTDOOR MODE	MEETING MODE	DRIVING MODE	SILENT MODE

Part 2

Practice the following expressions with your partners and try to write down your own sentences.

1. Let me welcome you to the first day of our annual meeting.

   Let me welcome you to_____.

2. I'd like to remind everyone to please switch your mobile phones to silent mode.

I'd like to remind everyone_____.

3. In your hands, you should have the agenda for today.

In your hands, you should have_____.

4. We will end this day with a happy hour in our employee lounge.

We will end this day with_____.

Unit 4-2 Introducing the Presenter 怎麼介紹主講人？

🎧 23

CEO: (*speaking*)

Thank you, Sarah.

Good morning, Colleagues. Again, welcome to Taipei. Many of you traveled a long way to be with us and I thank you for that.

In the past few years, all of us at Acme Inc. have worked hard to build outstanding products, provide exceptional service, and sustain our strong growth. We all expect the same commitment to excellence for many more years to come.

As part of our goal to build a better business, we entered into a partnership with the University of ABC at the end of last year. Sarah's team has been working with Professor Hank Green to improve our marketing strategies and their execution. As a faculty member and current dean of the marketing department, Professor Green has over 30 years of experience in teaching, research, and collaboration with multinational companies in Asia. Believe me when I say we have learned a lot from him. This morning, the three of us will share the results of our work with you and how they will shape our approach.

At the end of this morning's session, we'd like to hear your input and open up the floor for Q & A as well as comments.

So, without further delay, please let us welcome Professor Hank Green.

Activity 1 Listening practice

 24

Part 1

Listen to the CD carefully and answer the following questions. Play it as many times as you need.

Question 1: Where are the companies that Professor Green has collaborated with?
(A) Swam Valley.   (B) Violet Valley.
(C) Nicon Valley.   (D) Silicon Valley.

Question 2: What are the goals that the speaker mentioned?
(A) Marketing goals.   (B) Researching goals.
(C) Production goals.   (D) Health goals.

Question 3: According to the speaker, does the audience have to take notes?
(A) Yes.   (B) No.

(C) The speaker doesn't tell us.

Question 4: What is the speaker talking about?

(A) Introducing a guest speaker.

(B) Buying products.

(C) How to apply for a college.

(D) How to cooperate with your friends.

 25

Part 2

Listen to the CD carefully and fill in the blanks.

To build a better business, we (1)_____ into a partnership with the University of ABC at the end of last year. Sarah's (2)_____ ___has been working with Professor James Green to (3)_____ our marketing strategies and execution. As a faculty member and current dean of the marketing department, Professor Green has over (4)_____ __ experience in teaching, research and collaboration with multi-national companies (5)_____ Asia. This morning, the (6)_____ of us will share the results of our work with you and how they will shape our approach.

Activity 2 Discussion

1. To be a host or hostess in a meeting needs a lot of skills. Talk with your partners and make a list of what you need to put in your opening speech as a host or hostess. Then, practice and present with your partners.

2. In Taiwan, where and how can you learn how to be a good English speaker?

Activity 3 Understanding and applying words, idioms, and phrases

Part 1

Learn the following expressions and make your own sentences orally.

Useful expression	Definition	Application
colleague	同事	▪ Colleagues are people who work with you in the same place or company.
exceptional	例外的、特殊的	▪ Norman is an exceptional student in our school.
sustain	維持	▪ How can you sustain a healthy lifestyle if you eat junk food every day?
commitment	承諾、保證	▪ My boyfriend made a commitment to donate money to the poor.
partnership	合夥關係	▪ Three professors formed a partnership to write a research paper.
strategy	策略	▪ Our government's strategy is to keep living expenses down.
execution	執行、實行	▪ The execution of the plan will take a couple of weeks.
dean	主任	▪ The dean of our department comes from India.
collaboration	合作、共同研究	▪ Mike did the research in collaboration with his wife.

Part 2

Practice the following short speech as a host or hostess. Then, deliver it without looking at the script. Be sure to use your body language naturally.

Good evening! Ladies and gentlemen, it's my great honor to extend my hearty welcome to you all! Tonight we have bright twinkling stars in the sky and also here on this stage. We are delighted to have you here to participate and share your precious experience. We hope this meeting will make your long trip worthwhile. Now, put your hands together to welcome our keynote speaker, Dr. Wang.

Note:
The following website is for your reference.
How to prepare an opening address in 4 easy steps (by write-out-loud. com)
http://www.write-out-loud.com/welcome-speech.html

This is a small part of the keynote speech given by Professor Green in the meeting.

Thank you for the introduction, Morgan. It's nice to get such attention here.

First of all, I'd like to congratulate all of you on successful projects in the past year. The competition in this industry is fierce, but Acme has managed to stay ahead of the game. In working with Sarah and the Acme team, we've returned to the most fundamental question: What does the market want?

Thus, we begin the path to re-examine our marketing strategies. We gathered valuable information in key areas such as target market, competitor performance and lastly, current and future market environments. In essence, marketing research helps us determine whether to make adjustments and how to allocate our resources.

I understand that these are very general points, so with the help of Morgan and Sarah, we will begin our discussion with specifics. I also invite all of you to make comments and raise questions at the end of our time together. Of course, you may email them to us if you are shy or if we run out of time. The point is that your input is extremely valuable to us.

Activity 1 Listening practice

 26

Part 1

Choose the expression that is spoken in the recording.

1. The competition in this industry is fierce, but Acme has managed to___

   _____.

   (A) stay ahead of the game
   (B) stay above troubles
   (C) steadily win the game
   (D) steadily generate profits

2. In essence, marketing research helps us determine whether to make adjustments and how to_____.

   (A) collect our resources
   (B) manage our resources
   (C) allocate our resources
   (D) accept our resources

3. With the help of Morgan and Sarah, we will begin our discussion with

   _____.

   (A) general
   (B) generalization
   (C) specifics
   (D) specifications

4. Of course, you may email them to us if you are shy or if we_____.

   (A) run out of money
   (B) run out of time
   (C) run out of cash
   (D) run out of resources

5. The point is that your input is extremely_____to us.

   (A) expensive

   (B) important

   (C) manageable

   (D) valuable

Part 2

The above speech is just a simple example. For quality and interesting speeches, we encourage you to check out many full-length speeches by TED speakers https://www.ted.com/ . Below are TED talks on learning that we think you will be interested. While you listen, keep notes or draw a concept map to show how the talk is structured.

1. The first 20 hours -- how to learn anything by Josh Kaufman at TEDxCSU (19:26, in English).
https://www.YouTube.com/watch?v=5MgBikgcWnY
2. How to learn any language in six months by Chris Lonsdale at TEDxLingnanUniversity.
https://www.YouTube.com/watch?v=d0yGdNEWdn0
(18:25, in English)
https://www.YouTube.com/watch?v=BENA8QSPmLY
(35:31, in Chinese)

Activity 2 Discussion

The talks above are all about efficient learning. Do you agree that learning can be so efficient and quick? What is your own language learning experience like? For this activity, you will practice and present a three- to five-minute formal talk in front of the class in response to the speeches.

Activity 3 Understanding and applying words, idioms, and phrases

Useful expression	Definition	Application
manage to	設法	The company finally managed to keep their office in the new building.
stay ahead of the game	領先	The best way to stay ahead of the game is to work harder than anybody else.
marketing strategies	市場策略	We need new marketing strategies to increase sales.
target market	目標市場	In order to meet the needs of its target market, the restaurant hired many Chinese-speaking helpers.
In essence	基本上	In essence, all good things in life cost nothing at all.
to make adjustments	調整	It will take months before we can fully make adjustments to the design.
to allocate resources	分配資源	The management is expected to allocate resources fairly among all the departments.
general	籠統	Those suggestions John made in the meeting are too general to be useful.
with the help of	有…的幫助	The problem can be solved with the help of the IT team.
specifics	細節	If you can give me the specifics quickly, the product will be made correctly.

Useful expression	Definition	Application
make comments	提出看法	The mayor decided not to make any comments before next Monday.
raise questions	問問題	Please raise any questions that you may have.
run out of time	時間用完了	We must make the teacher understand our difficulties before we run out of time.

🎧 27

Sarah: At this point, let's open up the floor for Q & A.

Stacey: Hello Professor Green, sorry for my poor English. May I ask you a question?

Prof. Green: Of course! That's what we're here for. What's your name?

Stacey: Sorry, my name is Stacey.

Prof. Green: Hello, Stacey. First of all, your English is good. But more importantly, give yourself credit for having the guts to speak in front of many people. Now, what's your question?

Stacey: Thank you, Professor. Earlier, you mentioned the importance of being "in tune" with the market. Could you please explain that idea a little bit more? Thank you.

Prof. Green: Great question. I'll be happy to elaborate. The concept is simple but important: Companies should understand what customers want and need. Of course, this is an effort that requires the dedication of valuable human and financial resources.

Morgan: That's a good point, Professor. Frankly, at times, we are overly confident about our products. So, it's important to remind ourselves to be more in touch with the customer base and the market in general. Great companies are even able to anticipate market demands. That's our goal.

Prof. Green: I hope we have answered your question, Stacey.

Morgan: As Professor Green mentioned earlier, we encourage you to provide feedback and raise questions. Acme is our company, so it's upon all of us to drive its success.

Activity 1 Listening practice

28

Part 1
Fill in the blank as you listen to the audio recording.

Professor Lee: So far we have talked about stock market. Any question?

Student Ma: Sorry for my (1)_____ English. May I ask you a question?

Professor Lee: Sure! Go ahead!

Student Ma: What's the (2)_____ between bear market and bull market?

Professor Lee: Bear market is a special term for the stock market being in a (3)_____ trend, or a period of (4)_____ stock prices. This is the (5)_____ of a bull market. Bull market is when the stock market is in a period of (6) _____ stock prices.

29

Part 2
Listen to the CD and fill in the blanks based on what you hear.

That's a good point, Professor. Frankly, (1)_____, we are (2)___ _____confident about our products. So, it's important to (3)_____ _____ourselves to be more (4)_____the customer base and the market (5)_____. Great companies are even able to (6)_____market demands. That's our goal.

Activity 2 Discussion

Part 1

Asking questions is a skill that many language learners have problems with. In this activity, you have the opportunity to ask questions, and you can only answer others with more questions. Whoever gives a statement loses the game. Let's see how long you and your teammate can continue this question-only activity. Below is an example to help you get started:

: Do you want to go to a movie?

: What movie?

: Don't you remember how I told you about the movie 'Joy'?

: What about it?

: Have you ever thought about inventing something like a powerful mop?

: What!? Who would invent such a stupid thing?

: ... (*continue* ...)

Part 2

Discuss with your friends how you can ask questions to encourage a pleasant discussion with your visitors.

Activity 3 Understanding and applying words, idioms, and phrases

Useful expression	Definition	Application
give yourself credit for	給自己一點鼓勵	You need to give yourself some credit for being willing to try.
have the guts to	有勇氣	Somebody needs to have the guts to give the new boss some good suggestions.
elaborate	更進一步說明	The professor elaborated on her theory with an interesting example.
the dedication	投入	The young student's dedication to his study is highly encouraged.
human and financial resources	人事與財務資源	Over the years, our company has worked very hard to enrich our human and financial resources.
Frankly	老實說	Frankly, I have more questions than answers after his speech.
be in touch with	接近	The new model is definitely more in touch with the market than the previous one.
anticipate	期待	The students are happily anticipating the visit of the famous Japanese cartoonist.
It's upon all of us	靠我們所有人的努力	It's upon all of us to work hard and win the next game.

Chapter Five
Going Out After the Conference 會後出遊

Unit 5-1 **Going Out and Enjoying Ourselves**
訂出遊計劃

30

Aaron: Hey Karen!

Karen: Hi, Aaron.

Aaron: For once in my life, I really enjoyed the various talks and presentations in this annual meeting. This sounds strange, but I feel that I'm part of something big.

Karen: I have the same thoughts too! Ever since I joined this company, I feel that my efforts actually make a difference.

Aaron: It's a good feeling to know that we are appreciated and we have the opportunity to learn and grow.

Karen: I can't agree more!
Now, enough about work. A bunch of us from the office are going to Yong Kang Street for some food and drinks. Do you want to join us?

Aaron: Yeah, I would love to. Even though the meetings in the last few days were meaningful and interesting, I could really take a break too. So what's the plan?

Karen: Dumplings at Ding Tai Feng, of course! After that, I'll need to miraculously make room for some spicy beef noodles. As for drinks, we're not sure yet.

Aaron: Oh, man. That sounds wonderful. I know a small bar that's good for a big group.

Karen: Good.

Aaron: When are you guys heading out?

Karen: A few of us are heading back to the hotel to freshen up so we'll be ready in about 30 minutes.

Aaron: Okay. So, let's meet at 7:30 at Dongmen Station?

Karen: Perfect! I know exactly how to get there. See you soon.

Aaron: Bye for now.

Activity 1 Listening practice

30

Part 1

Listen to the CD and circle the correct answers based on what you hear.

Aaron: Hey Karen!

Karen: Hi Aaron.

Aaron: For once in my life, I really (enjoyed / joined) the various talks and presentations in this annual meeting. This sounds strange, but I feel that I'm part of something big.

Karen: I have the same (ideas /thoughts) too! Ever since I joined this company, I feel that my efforts actually make a difference.

Aaron: It's a good feeling to know that we are (agreed / appreciated) and we have the opportunity to learn and grow.

Karen: I can't agree more!

Now, enough about work. A bunch of us from the office are going to Yong Kang Street for some food and (🧁 drinks / 🍲 food). Do you want to join us?

Aaron: Yeah, I would love to. Even though the meetings in the last few days were meaningful and interesting, I could really take a (break / vacation) too. So what's the plan?

Karen: Dumplings at Ding Tai Feng, of course! After that, I'll need to miraculously make room for some spicy (chicken 🍗 / beef 🥩) noodles. As for drinks, we're not sure yet.

Aaron: Oh man. That sounds wonderful. I know a small bar that's good for a big group.

Karen: Good.

Aaron: When are you guys heading out?

Karen: A few of us are heading back to the hotel to (freshen / clean) up so we'll be ready in about 30 minutes.

Aaron: Okay. So, let's meet at 7:30 at Dongmen Station?

Karen: Perfect! I know (perfectly / exactly) how to get there. See you soon.

Aaron: Bye for now.

Part 2

Listen to the CD and circle the correct answers.

Question 1

 A.　 B.　 C.　 D.

32

Question 2

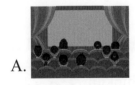 A.　 B.　 C.　 D.

Activity 2 Discussion

Where would you take your international visitors after a formal meeting if this is their first time in Taiwan? Discuss with your friends how to design a half-day, a one-day, or a two-day itinerary. Before you design, be sure to think about your visitor's backgrounds, such as their ages, preferences, and professions. Then, you need to present your itinerary and try to persuade your audience that yours is the best (such as most fun and economical).

Activity 3 Understanding and applying words, idioms, and phrases

Fill in the definitions of the following expressions.

Useful expression	Definition	Sentence making
1. annual meeting		• An annual meeting is a meeting which meets once in a year.
2. For once in my life, ...		• For once in my life, I was on time for the meeting.
3. Ever since		• Ever since Robert was bitten by a dog, he has hated dogs.
4. make a difference		• Your hard work will make a difference.
5. I can't agree more.		• A: Jay Chou is so cool. B: I can't agree more.
6. a bunch of us a bunch of money a bunch of grapes a bunch of roses ...		• Yesterday, a bunch of us went to explore a haunted / ghost house.

Useful expression	Definition	Sentence making
7. Even though ...		• I like Sean even though he is a troublemaker.
8. I would love to.		• I would love to read creative sentences written by my little brother Sean.
9. make room for		• There is an old lady over there. Would you please make room for her.
10. spicy beef noodles		• Wow, the spicy beef noodles almost killed me.
11. head out		• Are you ready to head out now? It's a little bit late.
12. freshen up		• I need to freshen up before going out.

5-2 **Enjoying the Night Market**
夜市，這是一定要的

33

Carrie and Bill are at the night market.

Carrie: Wow! What an incredible night market!

Bill: Pretty amazing, isn't it? The market is always extremely busy around this time at night.

Carrie: So, how do we attack this monster? I am not very confident about my ability to try new things.

Bill: Haha... no need to worry. I can steer you clear from the funky items like stinky tofu.

Carrie: No! I actually want to try it. You might have to finish the rest for me, though.

Bill: That's easy for me!

...Moments later...

Bill: Here you go. One order of stinky tofu.

Carrie: My god... How do I say this with the most respect? It smells pretty bad. I'm trying to convince myself that it tastes better than it smells.

Bill: If you think of it as cheese, you might feel better. It's a fermented food product much like cheese.

Carrie: Good idea. I'll imagine "fried cheese!" Here it goes. (*Chomp chomp*)

Bill: ... so... what do you think?

Carrie: Your suggestion really worked! I think I "psyched" myself out by thinking that it's slimy and gooey. In fact, it's actually pretty good. I think the crunchiness and the pickled vegetables are good combinations too.

Bill: I'm relieved to hear that. Now, how about we try some grilled chicken butts?

Carrie: Can't wait! Just kidding.

Bill: Come on. Let's get some fried dumplings, then.

Carrie: Bill, what's inside those dumplings?

Bill: Wait up.

Activity 1 Listening practice

For each of the pairs below, circle the particular words or expressions used by the speaker.

 33

1. Carrie: Wow! What an incredible (night market / market)!

2. Bill: Pretty amazing, isn't it? The market is always extremely busy around this time (at night / in the evening).

3. Carrie: So, how do we attack this market/monster? I'm not afraid of eating some (strange stuff / strange food).

4. Bill: Haha... no need to worry. I can steer you clear from the (funky

/ funny items) like stinky tofu.

5. Carrie: No! I actually want to try it. You might have to (finish the rest / do the rest) for me, though.

6. Bill: Will be glad to! That's easy for me.

...Moments later...

7. Bill: (There you are / Here you go). One order of stinky tofu.

8. Carrie: My god... It smells pretty bad. I'm trying to convince myself that it tastes better than it (smells / feels).

9. Bill: If you think of it as cheese, you might feel better. It's a fermented food product much like (cheese / ice cream).

10. Carrie: (Good idea / Great idea). I'll imagine "fried cheese!" Here it goes. (*Chomp chomp*)

11. Bill: ... so... (how do you feel / what do you think)?

12. Carrie: Your suggestion really worked! I think I "psyched" myself out by thinking that it's slimy and gooey. In fact, it's actually pretty good. I think the crunchiness and the pickled vegetables (cut the greasiness / are good combination) too.

13. Bill: I'm relieved to hear that. Now, how about we try some grilled chicken (butts / legs)?

14. Carrie: Can't wait! Just (kidding / killing).

15. Bill: Come on. Let's get some (fried dumplings / French fries), then.

16. Carrie: Bill, what's inside those dumplings?

17. Bill: (Wait for / Wait up).

Activity 2 Discussion

1. In addition to stinky tofu, what other food items from the night market can be considered "funky"?
2. Why is stinky tofu similar to cheese?
3. Besides food, what other merchandises can you get at night markets in Taiwan?

Activity 3 Understanding and applying words, idioms, and phrases

Part 1

Make sure that you understand all of the expressions below. Say them several times. Create and perform a 2-minute dialogue/skit with your partner using as many of the following expressions as possible.

1. How do we attack this monster?
2. I am trying to convince myself that ... (finish this sentence with your own words.) ...
3. Your suggestion really worked!
4. I'm relieved to hear that.
5. Can't wait!
6. Just kidding.

Part 2

Familiarize yourself with the following expressions:

1. attack this monster
2. funky items
3. fermented food products
4. psych myself out
5. slimy and gooey
6. crunchiness

Chapter Six
Getting to Know More About You 介紹你自己

Unit 6-1 **Chatting About Your Family** 聊聊你的家人

🎧 34

At the concert hall…

Dennis: Professor Green, the announcer just reminded the audience that the concert will begin in 10 minutes and we should turn off our cell phones.

Professor Green: Oh yes. I almost forgot. Let me put my phone on mute. So tell me more about your family, Dennis. Does your family live in Taipei?

Dennis:	Actually, my grandparents, parents and I all live together. Oh, and our dog, Cookie.
Professor Green:	Really? Is that still a common arrangement?
Dennis:	It's less so in Taipei, but still quite common for three generations of Taiwanese to live under the same roof. Sometimes, even four!
Professor Green:	Huh, That's amazing. How do you like it?
Dennis:	You might be surprised but I love it. My parents and grandparents adore having me around and I feel so pampered by them. They accuse me of only staying around for their cooking and cleaning. I can't agree more. Heh ...
Professor Green:	From the way you described it, I can imagine such a loving home. Did you ever think about moving out?
Dennis:	Not really. They really respect my space, that's why we have a good relationship. We live in a remodeled two-story condo, so there's plenty of room. Besides, I won't always have a chance to be near them.
Professor Green:	That's an interesting perspective. You are very lucky.
Dennis:	Yeah, I'm extremely blessed. Oh, here comes the conductor.
Professor Green:	I'm so excited about the concert. Thanks again for inviting me.

Activity 1 Listening practice

Listen to the CD and put the letters in the blanks with the correct order.

 35

(A) My parents and grandparents adore having me around and I feel so pampered by them.

(B) That's why I don't think of moving out.

(C) Actually, my grandparents, parents and I all live together.

(D) My family and I live in Taipei.

(E) I'm a lucky guy, I think.

(F) Besides, we live in a remodeled two-story condo, so there's plenty of room --- and they respect my space.

(G) I can't agree more.

(H) I love the way we live together.

(I) They accuse me of only staying around for their cooking and cleaning.

(J) That's why we have a good relationship.

(K) It's a less common arrangement in big cities, but still quite common for three generations of Taiwanese to live under the same roof.

1. _____ 2. _____ 3. _____ 4. _____ 5. _____ 6. _____ 7. _____ 8. _____ 9. _____
10. _____ 11. _____

Activity 2 Discussion

1. What kind of house do you live in? Condo (apartment) or house?
2. Describe the place you live. (How many floors, how many rooms, etc.)
3. Who do you live with? Do you prefer living alone or living with others? Why?

Activity 3 Understanding and applying words, idioms, and phrases

Part 1

Try to understand the transformation of the words and phrases. Then work in pairs to practice makeing more similar sentences.

1. a house with two stories → a two-story house
2. remodel(v.) a condo → a remodeled(pp.-->adj.) condo →
   a remodeled two-story condo

Example: My family lives in a remodeled two-story condo.

Part 2

Create a short dialogue using the following expressions.

- Turn off our cell phones.
- Put my phone on mute
- How do you like it?
- accuse me of ...
- staying around for ...
- I can't agree more.
- Did you ever think about moving out?
- a remodeled two-story condo
- Here comes the conductor.

Unit 6-2 Chatting About Your Favorites
聊聊你最愛的消遣活動

Ray and Grant are chatting outside the conference hall.

36

Grant: Hey Ray, how about taking a break from booth duty today? The trade show crowd is dying down so I think the assistants can handle the visitors by themselves.

Ray: That's a good idea. Let's get some fresh air.

(*Outside the convention center*)

Grant: So, tell me, with your busy work life, what do you like to do outside the office?

Ray: It's nothing exciting, but I like to go to the local sports center a few times a week.

Grant: Oh yeah? What do you do there?

Ray: Yeah. The sports center is run by the city and it's pretty inexpensive. I usually swim but if the weather is nice, I'll jog around the track.

Grant: Exercising is a great way to keep up the energy level in the daytime. I also try to work out as often as I can.

Ray: My wife joins me sometimes, but it depends on her schedule. Our favorite thing to do is to go for a walk after dinner. It gives us some time to catch up with each other.

Grant: Mmm, That's kind of romantic, Ray. I didn't know this side of you. What do you usually do on weekends?

Ray: Let's see ... Our weekends are usually filled with a little bit of everything like doing chores around the house and hanging out with family or friends. Recently, we and some friends have started hiking.

Grant: Ah, I think I've seen the pictures that you posted on Facebook. Some of those trails are stunning.

Ray: If you like, you're welcome to join us.

Grant: That sounds like fun. I'll be sure to tag along when I return to Taiwan next time. Oh, we better get back before the assistants start getting nervous.

Ray: You're right. Let's head back.

Activity 1 Listening practice

Circle the words you hear.

🎧 36

Grant: Hey Ray, how about taking a (bread / break) from booth duty? The trade show crowd is (dying / trying) down so I think the assistants can (candle / handle) the visitors by themselves.

Ray: That's a good idea. Let's get some fresh air.

(Outside the convention center)

Grant: So, tell me, with your busy work life, what do you like to do (outside / inside) the office?

Ray: It's nothing (interesting / exciting), but I like to go to the local sports center a few times a week.

Grant: Oh yeah? What do you do there?

Ray: Yeah. The sports center is run by the city and it's pretty (inexpensive / expensive). I usually swim but if the weather is nice, I'll (jog / walk) around the track.

Grant: Exercising is a great way to keep up the energy level in the daytime. I also try to work out as (often / usually) as I can.

Ray: My wife joins me sometimes, but it depends on her (plan / schedule). Our favorite thing to do is to go for a walk after dinner. It gives us some time to (catch / get) up with each other.

Grant: That's kind of romantic, Ray. I didn't know this side of you. What do you usually do on (weekdays / the weekend)?

Ray: More of the same. Just kidding.

Let's see ... our weekends are usually filled with a little bit of everything like doing chores around the house and (hanging / taking) out with family or friends. (Recently / Secretly), we and some friends have started hiking.

Grant: I think I've seen pictures that you posted on Facebook. Some of those trails are (surprising / stunning).

Ray: If you like, you're welcome to join us.

Grant: That sounds like fun. I'll be sure to (tag / bag) along when I return to Taiwan next time. Oh, we better get back before the assistants start getting nervous.

Ray: You're right. Let's (hand / head) back.

Activity 2 Discussion

1. What do you usually do on the weekend? Do you go out or stay at home?

2. Have you ever been to a sports center? Please describe one near you. What kind of facilities do they have? What do you usually do there?

3. Describe a kind of sport that you do most often or you enjoy the most. Chat with your friends as if you were chatting with an international visitor.

Activity 3 Understanding and applying words, idioms, and phrases

Part 1
Useful expressions

Useful expression	Definition
1. dying down	逐漸消失
2. It's nothing exciting.	沒有什麼令人興奮的事。
3. a few times a week	一週幾次
4. as often as I can	我盡量〔做〕
5. catch up with each other	跟上彼此的進度
6. More of the same.	都差不多。
7. Just kidding.	開玩笑的。
8. hanging out with family or friends	跟家人還有朋友常去何處逛逛閒扯
9. That sounds like fun.	聽起來很有趣。
10. tag along	跟隨
11.head back	回去

Part 2

Match the statements on the left with those on the right. This can be a competition among friends or in a class.

1. The crowd is dying down.

   (A) It's healthier to cook by ourselves than eating out.

2. Just kidding.

   (B) That's a lot !

3. I will tag along next time I visit Tainan.

   (C) I thought you were serious.

4. I eat at home as often as I can.

   (D) What makes you say that?

5. My work in the new company is more of the same.

   (E) Sure, I am a bit tired as well.

6. I enjoy hanging out with my family and friends during summer vacation.

   (F) Oh, that sounds boring.

7. It's nothing exciting.

   (G) Sure, it will be fun !

8. We have to catch up with each other at least three times a week.

   (H) That's because it is getting dark.

9. That sounds like fun !

   (I) Yes, it is ! Do you want to join?

10. Let's head back to the hotel.

    (J) What do you do when you are with them?

Unit 6-3 Dining at Home 請他回家吃飯

Karen is invited to Aaron's home and to have dinner with Aaron's family.

🎧37

Aaron: Please sit, Karen. My Mom says you should make yourself at home and not be shy. The more you eat, the happier she is.

Karen: That's so sweet, Aaron. Thank you. Mr. and Mrs. Hong, "hsieh hsieh!" Please tell your parents that this feast looks amazing and that I'm throwing my etiquette out the window!

Aaron: Good! I've been craving some home cooking all semester now. Finally, thanks to your visit, I get to enjoy mama's cooking too.

Karen: I don't want to be rude, but could you tell me about the dishes? Don't worry, I am very adventurous.

Aaron: Haha... sorry to disappoint you.
These are common dishes but every mom has her unique flavor. Besides the stir-fry vegetables, it looks like my mom prepared delicious steamed pork ribs with gravy, scrambled eggs with tomatoes and some braised bean curd. If you're looking for pig-

blood cake or stinky tofu, we'll have to stop by the night market tomorrow.

Karen: Wow, I don't think I've had any of these dishes. What are the pork ribs like?

Aaron: Hmm... They're ribs that are cut up in smaller pieces then marinated in garlic, ginger, and other spices. Instead of baking or smoking them, the dish is traditionally steamed. The gravy is on the watery side, but it is so good over rice.

In Chinese cooking, there is a lot of stir-frying as well as steaming. A good cook will have a repertoire of techniques and go-to dishes. Trust me, you won't find what you see tonight at a night market.

Karen: Mmmm~ I can't wait to start!

Aaron: Good call. My Mom asked me to stop talking.

Mrs. Hong: 開動！(*Mrs. Hong gestures digging in!*)

Karen: I like the sound of that.

Activity 1 Listening practice

Now you should practice on your own. When you are so familiar with the expressions that they would appear in your talk without much effort they are of course yours.

Suggestions for practice

- With a friend: You can find a friend and roleplay with him/her.
- On your own: Play the two roles on your own at the same time.
- Use an audio recorder: You could also audio record one role, and then try to play the second role in person.

We are sure you could come up with your own creative ways to practice. All in all, the tip is that you have to really enjoy the practice.

Activity 2 Discussion

Study carefully again how Aaron explains his mother's dish:

(Turn 5) Aron: ...*a delicious steamed pork rib with gravy...*

(Turn 7) Aron: *Hmm... They're ribs that are cut up in smaller pieces then marinated in garlic, ginger, and other spices. Instead of baking or smoking them, the dish is traditionally steamed...*

Most dishes could not be understood by names, unless the person has already tried them. For example, there is a Taiwanese dish which can be translated literally as 'Buddha Jumping Over the Wall.' This is a dish that many families have at the Chinese new year festival. People would not understand what you are talking about if they have never seen it, even if you speak Chinese and they understand Chinese. You have to give more description focusing on the cooking technique, ingredient, shape, taste, stories, or cultural information. This will give you a lot of things to chat about with your international visitors.

Does your family have some unique dishes? Are there any popular dishes around your campus? Please use the words in the table below to describe one cuisine and see if your partner understands what you are talking about. Do not try to translate the Chinese term. Follow Aaron's example and be really descriptive and informative.

You've got to try it!!

Activity 3 Understanding and applying words, idioms, and phrases

Part 1

Familiarize yourself with the following useful expressions and make your own sentences.

Useful expression	Definition	Application
1. make yourself at home	請不要拘束	• Make yourself at home.
2. etiquette	禮儀	• The book with the red cover is on etiquette.
3. crave for	渴望	• I crave for more speaking experience.
4. Thanks to…	幸虧	• Thanks to her help, I finished my job in time.
5. adventurous	冒險的	• My brother is an adventurous man who is not afraid of taking risks.
6. marinate	醃泡	• Chinese people like marinated chicken feet.
7. repertoire	可表演的節目	• There are hundreds of songs in the musician's repertoire.
8. go-to dishes	喜歡、方便、常吃的菜	• What are your basic go-to dishes?

go-to ...的用法很多

※go-to …拿手、喜歡

1. go-to restaurant

2. go-to method

3. go-to drink (favorite beverage)

   When my guests are hot and thirsty, my <u>go-to beverage</u> to serve them is a cold glass of lemonade.

4. go-to pair of pants

   When I am going on a long business trip, my <u>go-to pair of pants</u> is my wrinkle free khakis because they are comfortable and need no ironing.

※go-to…解決困境的方法，也就是想都不用想的所謂「口袋法門」：

Your go-to 'X' is the 'X' that you will resort to most commonly when you don't have the inclination/tie to come up with something more original, or else that you will just go to automatically.

Part 2

Culture Study

In the Taiwanese context we would address other people's parents as uncles or aunties, but is this appropriate if they are from a different country? How do you address your friends' parents if you have a chance to meet them or if you are invited to their homes? How do you say 吃素 in English? If somebody says "it's interesting," do they mean they like it? Discuss these questions with your friends.

Chapter Seven
Sharing Our Cultures 分享自己的文化

Unit 7-1 Taking up Native Dialects
閒聊家族語言背景

Natalie, Karen and Bill are having coffee while chatting.

38

Natalie: I'm really impressed by the progress you have made with your Mandarin.

Karen: Thanks! I mean xie xie! (謝謝！) Being here for a longer period of time really helped me pick up more Chinese. But, I still have no luck learning Taiwanese, though.

Bill: Actually, you're not alone. So many young people are unable to speak the dialect of their parents and grandparents. They may understand it but they have a hard time speaking it.

Karen: Really?

Natalie: Yeah, it's true. For instance, my father's parents are from Guangdong Province where people mainly speak Cantonese. My mother's family has been in Taiwan for many generations and they speak Taiwanese.

Naturally, my parents are fluent in the dialects of their elders, but I am not.

Karen: That's really too bad. Are these dialects not spoken enough?

Bill: For me, I understand the Hakka dialect, but I just can't really put my thoughts into words. This is what I think happened. With Mandarin being the main language taught and spoken in our schools, children return home not used to speaking their mother tongue. So from the lack of practice, the ability to speak it is lost.

Natalie: I agree with Bill. Our dialects have been ignored by our school curriculum for a long time. We have such a diverse mix of people from all over China and incredibly rich indigenous cultures. However, because of the cultural and political complexities of our past, fewer and fewer people in our generation are able to communicate in those beautiful words.

Bill: Of course, we can't just blame the government or schools. That would be simplifying the issue. What we do at home is also an important element of learning too.

Karen: I understand what you mean. My mother is from Russia but I can only understand Russian; I get tongue tied when I try to form simple sentences.

Bill: Now, I'm less embarrassed. Seriously, though, I'm glad that our schools are dedicating more resources to teaching kids regional dialects and native cultures. There are also educational programs on TV with this mission too.

Karen: That's really great to hear. Ultimately, I think small changes can begin within us. Hey, I know! How about you two teach me something besides Mandarin today?

Both: That sounds fun!

Notes:

Guangdong is also known as Canton, so the language spoken by the people in that region is called "Cantonese."

Taiwanese dialect (台灣閩南語) is a Hokkien dialect spoken by people in Fujian Province, Taiwan and throughout Southeast Asia.

Activity 1 Listening practice

39

Part 1

Listen to the CD and answer the following questions.

1. Where does the speaker's father come from?
    (A) Taiwan.   (B) Canton.
    (C) Tailand.   (D) Shanghai.
2. Where does the speaker's mother come from?
    (A) Taiwan.   (B) Canton.
    (C) Tailand.   (D) Shanghai.
3. Which dialect does the speaker can speak more than others?
    (A) Mandarin.   (B) Cantonese.
    (C) Taiwanese.   (D) Shanghai dialect.

40

Part 2

Listen to the CD and circle the correct answers.

Our dialects have been ignored by our school (1) (curricular / curriculum) for a long time. We have such a (2) (diverse / dive) mix of people from all over China and from incredibly rich indigenous cultures. However, (3) (because /because of) the cultural and political complexities of our past, fewer and fewer people in our (4) (generator / generation) are able to communicate in those beautiful words. Of course, we can't just (5) (blend / blame) the government or schools. That would be simplifying the issue. What we do at home is also an important (6) (elementary / element) of learning too.

Now, I'm glad that our schools are dedicating more resources in teaching kids regional dialects and (7) (native / naive) cultures. There are also educational programs on TV (8) (with / of) this mission too. Little by little, our dialects can be kept.

Activity 2 Discussion

1. What's the difference between language and dialect?
2. Besides Mandarin, what other dialects can you speak? If you can, please say something in a dialect to your partners and see if they can get the meaning.
3. Can you speak your grandparents' dialects? Why or why not?

Activity 3 Understanding and applying words, idioms and phrases

Part 1
Useful expressions
Learn the following expressions and practice making your own sentences. If necessary, use your smartphone to check the usage.

- pick up Chinese 不經心地就學會中文了
- put my thought into words 將思想轉換爲語言
- agree with 同意
- diverse 多種多樣的
- indigenous 本土的
- simplify 簡單化
- element 元素
- get tongue tied 舌頭打結
- regional 地區性的

Part 2

Patterns

The following patterns are commonly used. Be sure to know how to use them.

1. With···,

    With a lot of books in my arms, I can't hold a strap on the bus.

    With (drinking) a lot of beer, I was kind of tipsy, walking on the street.

2. Though

    • Being here for a longer period of time really helped me pick up more Chinese. I still have no luck learning Taiwanese, **though.** = **Though** being here for a longer period of time really helped me pick up more Chinese, I still have no luck learning Taiwanese.

    • Seriously, **though**, I'm glad that our schools are dedicating more resources in teaching kids regional dialects and native cultures.

More practice:

I love him. My parents don't like him, **though**.

→My parents don't like him **though** I love him.

→**Though** I love him, my parents don't like him.

→I love him, **but** my parents don't like him.

Unit 7-2 Learning Some Chinese Expressions
教他幾句簡單華語

Aaron joins Karen and Carrie at a bar.

🎧 41

Carrie: This is a really cool bar, Aaron. How long have you been coming here?

Aaron: This is only my second time. When Karen invited me earlier, I immediately thought of this place.

Karen: Good choice, my friend. This drink is so refreshing on a warm evening. Look, I have almost finished it!

Carrie: We'll need to order another one for Karen. How do you say one more?

Aaron: "Zai lai yi bei, xie xie". Literally, that means one more glass, thank you.

Carrie: "Zai lai yi bei, xie xie". Let me try it now. Before I learned this phrase, I only make eye contact with the server and point to my glass.

Karen: How cool! Seems like what a mysterious character would do in a detective novel.

Carrie: "Xie xie." (All laughing) Just kidding. I'm anything but cool.

Karen: I think saying "bu hao yi si" goes a long way when I'm trying to get directions or flagging down a waiter.

Carrie: That's a pretty good approach. Even if you know only a few words, making the effort to speak the language really make the other person know that you're trying.

Aaron: And, it shows respect and sincerity. That's big in Taiwanese culture.

Karen: I know! Let's make Carrie order for us from now on. You need to practice.

Carrie: "Deng y xia!" I'm not so sure about this proposal.

Notes:

Zai lai yi bei, xie xie	再來一杯，謝謝
Xie xie	謝謝
Bu hao yi si	不好意思
Deng yi xia	等一下

Activity 1 Listening practice

 42

Part 1

Listen to the CD and answer the following questions.

1. Where is this conversation taking place?
    (A) At a coffee shop.   (B) At a bar.
    (C) At a convenience store.   (D) At a concert hall.
2. What does the man order for the woman?
    (A) Orange juice.   (B) Latte.
    (C) Espresso.   (D) Milk tea.
3. Why does the man take the woman to this place?
    (A) It is close to their place.   (B) Drinks here are cheaper.
    (C) The decorations are good.   (D) The atmosphere is good.

Listen to the CD and fill in the blanks.

 43

Part 2

Karen: This drink is so (4)_____. Look, I have almost finished it!

Carrie: We'll need to order another one for Karen. How do you say one more?

Aaron: "Zai lai yi bei, xie xie", (5)_____ means one more glass, thank you.

Carrie: "Zai lai yi bei, xie xie". Let me try it now. Before I learned this phrase, I only (6)_____and point to my glass.

Karen: "How cool!" Seems like what a mysterious character (7)_____ in a detective novel.

Carrie: Xie xie. (All laughing) Just kidding. I'm anything but cool.

Karen: I think saying "bu hao yi si" goes a long way when I'm trying to get directions or (8)_____ a waiter.

Carrie: That's a pretty good approach. Even if you know only a few words, you try your best to (9)_____and really let the other person know that you're trying.

Aaron: And, it shows respect and sincerity. That's big in (10)_____ culture.

Karen: I know! Let's make Carrie (11)_____for us from now on. You need to practice.

Carrie: "Deng yi xia!" I'm not so sure about this proposal.

Activity 2 Discussion

Do you have the experience of teaching Chinese to foreign friends? If you have the chance, which expressions will you teach them first? Why?

Activity 3 Understanding and applying words, idioms, and phrases

Learn the following expressions. Then work in pairs to make your own sentences.

※think of 想到

When I think of Heads Up, I think of Ellen.

※make eye contact with 眼神接觸

When you make a speech, you should have eye contact with the audience.

※anything but 絕對不

anything but cool. → not cool

anything but ordinary → not ordinary

anything but well-educated → not well-educated

Jackie is anything but creative.

※go a long way → spend a lot of time用（花）很長時間、成功

    For a beginner to speak English goes a long way.

※to flag down 揮手攔

    flag down a passing car

    hail a passing car

    Freda flagged down a taxi in the middle of the night.

※making (the) efforts to 盡力

    Jackie Chen made efforts to practice martial arts when he was young.

※That's big in Taiwanese culture. 以台灣文化來說，這是很重要的。

44

Natalie and Carrie are arriving at Longshan Temple by the MRT.

Natalie: Here we are, Carrie. This is Longshan Temple.

Carrie: What a beautiful place!

Natalie: Pretty awesome, isn't it?

Carrie: It is so grand! I can really feel the history of this temple.

Natalie: Longshan Temple is one of the oldest temples in Taiwan. For generations, it brought a sense of peace and hope to people. Notice the light smoke over there?

Carrie: How can I miss it? I have always loved the mystique of burning incense. Maybe the smoke carries our messages to the gods.

Natalie: That's a really nice thought.

Carrie: Thanks.
Is there a party later? I see so many people put food and beverages on those tables.

Natalie: No, those are offerings to the gods. My grandma said, "When you feed the gods, they are happy so they make sure you are safe."

Carrie: So it's a type of bribery?

Natalie: HAHA. I would say so. But I think it's a way to help humans feel less anxious about their worries and fears.

Carrie: Mm... That makes sense. What are they doing over there by the altar?

Natalie: Good question! They are doing "bwa bwei" with divination blocks.

Often, people turn to the gods for answers when faced with difficult decisions in life. They receive the response from the way the blocks land on the floor.

Carrie: That's so cool. Can I try?

Natalie: Yes, of course. But you must be sincere in your belief and question. After this, I'll show you something else.

Carrie: Great! This is a very interesting experience.

Natalie: You know, Longshan Temple is only one of thousands of temples in Taiwan. You won't be able to see them all, but now you have a good understanding.

Carrie: You're right about that. I'm so glad we came here.

Notes:

1. bwa bwei 擲筊
2. divination blocks 筊杯

Activity 1 Listening practice

 45

Part 1

Listen to the CD and fill in the blanks.

Natalie: Let's take MRT (1)_____Line to Longshan Temple.

Carrie: At which station should we get off?

Natalie: Longshan Temple (2)_____.

Carrie: Great, it's good to (3)_____.

(*getting off the train*)

Natalie: Look! This is Longshan Temple.

Carrie: What a (4)_____place!

Natalie: Pretty awesome, isn't it?

Carrie: It is so grand! I can really feel the history of this temple.

Natalie: Longshan Temple is one of the oldest (5)_____
in Taiwan. For generations, it brought a (6)_____
of peace and hope to people. Notice the light smoke over there?

Carrie: How can I miss it? I have always loved the mystique of
(7)_____. Maybe the smoke (8)_____our messages
to the gods.

Natalie: That's a really nice thought.

Carrie: Thanks.

46

Part 2

Listen to the CD and answer the questions.

1. How many names of temples are mentioned?

    (A) 1   (B) 2   (C) 3   (D) 4

2. How old is Tianhou Temple?

    (A) Over 100 years old.   (B) Over 200 years.

    (C) Over 300 years old.   (D) Over 400 years.

3. What was the main purpose of the temples when they were first built
    in Taipei?

    (A) A place of worship.   (B) A place of burning incense.

    (C) A place for settlers.   (D) A place of arts.

Activity 2 Discussion

1. Can you introduce "bwa bwei" with divination blocks? Please
   introduce the procedure to a friend in English.
2. Can you introduce religions in Taiwan? How many are there? How
   many temples are there in Taiwan? How many belong to Buddhism
   and how many belong to Taoism?

Activity 3 Understanding and applying words, idioms and phrases

Part 1

Try to learn the following words and make your own sentences with a partner.

Useful expression	Definition	Application
1. awesome	令人驚嘆的	Your performance at school is awesome.
2. grand	雄偉的	Today is the grand opening of Cat Department Store. They are offering 20% discount.
3. mystique	神秘色彩	There is a mystique about eating dog meat.
4. incense	香	My grandma doesn't like the smell of the burning incense.
5. beverage	飲料	Beverages are not allowed on the MRT.
6. offerings	捐獻物	People make offerings of money to help remodel the church.
7. altar	祭壇	This altar is decorated like a wedding party full of flowers.
8. response	回應	Mr. Anderson's response was not accepted.
9. sincere	真誠	Eric's sincere attitude won his homeroom teacher's heart.

Part 2

Pair work. Within 2 minutes, the one who can make more sentences based on the above words will be the winner. You may use a stopwatch or the stopwatch function of your smartphone

Part 3

Form a group of 3 or 4. Write down what you can see in a temple and read them out loud. Be sure that the pronunciation of each word is correct.

（筊杯）	（香）
（廟口大門）	（貢桌）
（神明）	（貢品）
（算命仙）	（冥紙）
（跪凳）	（香客）

APPENDIX 附錄
附錄一：課文翻譯、解答與深入學習資料

 Chapter One: Arrival 初來乍到

Unit 1-1 **Email Exchange** 怎麼寫Email聯絡才不失禮

前言：招待國外訪客參加主辦會議，在很早之前就得做很多聯繫，比方得連絡演講者，通常是在業界有名氣的大師級人物，而且常用email。寫email跟一般書信比較像的地方是它禮貌周到，但又不失商業書信講究效率的特色。本單元就以兩封email為主題，先是奧斯卡給受邀的葛林教授，另一封是葛林教授的回信。

本文翻譯

葛林教授和奧斯卡間的email對談。奧斯卡用Dear稱呼教授，而教授用Hi對奧斯卡說，感覺出兩者的不同嗎？

親愛的葛林教授：

　　謝謝您傳來的班機和旅館資訊。我會親自到機場迎接。請尋找有您名字的牌子。

　　如您有任何對住宿上的特殊需求的話，煩請告訴我。我很樂意為您作安排。

　　我們工程部門的所有員工都對您的來訪很興奮，同時也很期待與您見面。祝您旅途愉快！

誠摯的問候
奧斯卡・李
Acme, Inc.（所屬公司名）

嗨，奧斯卡：

　　謝謝您跟我在機場會面。非常感激。我不需要任何東西，只要在赴旅館途中買些當地的食物即可。假如方便的話，請帶我到傳統早餐店。我期待與您和您的同事見面。

誠摯的問候

漢克・葛林

ABC大學機械工程教授

Activity 1 Listening practice

01

1. ___C___ 2. ___A___ 3. ___F___ 4. ___E___ 5. ___B___ 6. ___G___
7. ___D___

02

1. ___D___ 2. ___B___ 3. ___E___ 4. ___A___ 5. ___C___

Activity 2 Discussion

　　這兩封email表面上都由三個主要部分組成，你可以回到本文看，請問是哪三部分？為什麼要有這三部分？你發出去的email也都有這三部分嗎？

開頭問候	本文	結尾署名
(Greetings and Introduction)	(Body)	(Conclusion and Signature)

Activity 3 Understanding and applying words, idioms, and phrases

Part 1

　　上面兩封email真的都還滿注重禮貌的，那我們就從學習怎麼表達禮貌開始吧！下面的表格裡，左邊是原文，右邊是延伸練習，請大家好好研究一下這些句子到底是怎麼構成的（注意劃底線的部分），然後請再多造幾個類似的句子。

原文	延伸練習
1. 謝謝您把您飛機航班及飯店的資訊寄給我。謝謝您友善的表達。	• Thank you for the ride.
2. 真的很感謝。	• I really appreciate your company.
3. 請尋找寫著您名字的牌子。	• Please try some cookies.
4. 如果您有任何住宿〔方面〕特殊的需求，請告訴我。	• If you have any special requests for food, please let me know.
5. 如果不麻煩的話，就帶我去一家對你比較方便的早餐店吧。	• If it's no trouble, please help me get a bigger hotel room.
6. 我別的都不需要，只想去傳統早餐店吃點當地的食物。	• I don't need anything other than a bigger hotel room.
7. 我很樂意〔為您〕做安排。	• I will be happy to show you around.
8. 我們都很期待見到您本人。	• I look forward to showing you around.
9. 祝您有個愉快的旅程。	• Have a great trip!

Part 2

我們可不能停在書寫造句而已喔，接著我們要真正說出口並運用出來。一定要很熟練，這裡的九宮格活動才做得起來：四人一組，輪流抽一到九的號碼。抽到號碼，先把格子中的原文唸出來，然後再造一個類似的句子；最好一面說，一面把聲音、表情都做出來，表達你的誠意。經同伴（或老師）認可，最早完成一條線的人，就贏得了一局！然後請繼續努力，一定要有禮貌喔！

深入學習參考資料

利用本單元所提供的寫作email寫三部分練習，繼續努力。以下提供對學習寫email有幫助的網路資料，第一個是文字資料，第二個是影音解說，全都是英文資料，讓你以讀與聽的方式學習email寫作。

1. 不可思議的絕妙好email到底是怎麼寫的？

An Editor's Guide to Writing Ridiculously Good Emails. http://www.forbes.com/sites/dailymuse/2013/11/19/an-editors-guide-to-writing-ridiculously-good-emails/

網頁出現後請按右上角Continue to Site，因為網頁效果阻礙，建議直接用Google找An Editor's Guide to Writing Ridiculously Good Emails. 文中關於寫一封讓對方留下好印象的email，提出三個重點：

- Make Sure it Has a Beginning, Middle, and End 要有前中後三個部份（也就是，先要有greetings 問候一下，引入正題，然後有結語）。
- Proofread and Fact Check 確實檢查文字與資料之正確。
- Think How You Would Feel if it Went Public 想一下如果這封信流傳出去後果會如何，你能承擔嗎？

2. 五大email常見結尾用語5 Useful Email Expressions (by Learn English with Emma) https://www.YouTube.com/watch?v=itLLVAJjXNI

(1) **Please find attached** _____ (e.g., photos from the conference). 隨函謹附（某文件檔案）（例如會議照片）。

(2) **I am forwarding** _____ **to you** (e.g., **an itinerary** of Professor Green's trip to Taiwan). 隨函謹把某文件檔案轉給你（例如格林教授的旅程明細表，forward的意思，是他寄來給我的，現在轉寄給你）。

(3) **I've cc'd/cc'ed/added** (a name) **on this email.** 我也同時讓某人收到這email。（Keep someone in the loop. 讓他知道一下。）

(4) **If you have any questions, please don't hesitate to contact me.** 若有任何疑問，隨時歡迎與我聯絡。

(5) **I look forward to** _____ (e.g., your visit to Taiwan/hearing from you/meeting you/your reply). **期待**你的台灣行／期待收到你的回訊／期待與你見面／期待你的回答）。

(6) 最後在你的名字前面再寫**Kind regards,** 或者**Regards,** 或者**Warm wishes,** 或**Yours truly.** 像本課中他們兩位這樣，後面應該再放職階與所屬公司（全部放在左邊即可）。

Regards,
Hank Green
Professor of Mechanical Engineering
University of ABC

Unit 1-2 Meeting at the Airport
機場接機，訪客會問你什麼問題？

前言：機場接機，還滿有挑戰性的。一來是你跟訪客不熟，離開機場後一路上要找到適當的話聊天，不容易啊！二來你可能對自己的國家、學校、或任職機構也不很清楚，更何況是得以英文回答問題。好，這一課就以Oscar接機展開！

本文翻譯

葛林教授：嗨，〈伸出手來握手〉我是漢克‧葛林。你一定就是奧斯卡。

　奧斯卡：嗨，葛林教授〈伸出手來握手〉。是的，我是奧斯卡。

葛林教授：很高興見到你，奧斯卡。謝謝你來接我。

奧斯卡：這是我的榮幸。看起來好像您的行李都到齊了。這邊請。大樓外面有車在等我們。您飛過來這一路上還好吧？

葛林教授：著陸的時候有點顛頗，不過航程大致很順利。只是我沒辦法在飛機上進食，因為噪音太大等等。我現在還真有點餓了！

奧斯卡：好啊，讓我們離開這裡去吃早餐。去個像樣的地方吃如何？

葛林教授：謝謝，沒關係。我只要在飯店的咖啡廳隨便吃吃。我想在會議前，你一定有很多事要辦吧。

奧斯卡：一點都不麻煩。何況我也需要吃啊。

葛林教授：好！這樣的話你介意我們吃點中式油條和燒餅嗎？

奧斯卡：了解！我知道有個好地方。

葛林教授：太棒了！謝謝，奧斯卡。我餓扁了。

Activity 1 Listening practice

04

Part 1

1. Green: Hi. (I'm) Hank Green. (J) <u>You must be Oscar</u>.
2. Oscar: Hi, Professor Green. Yes, I am Oscar.
3. Green: Very nice to meet you, Oscar. (E) <u>Thank you for picking me up</u>.
4. Oscar: It's my pleasure.

Part 2

5. Oscar: (C) <u>It looks like you have all your bags</u>. Let's get out of here and have some breakfast. (G) <u>How about I take you some place decent</u>.
6. Green: Thank you, but that's OK. (K) <u>I'll grab a quick bite in the hotel cafe</u>. I'm sure you have plenty of things to finish up before the conference.
7. Oscar: (A) <u>It's no trouble at all</u>. Plus, I have to eat too.

8. Green: (D) <u>In that case</u>, do you mind if we get some Chinese donuts and the flaky sesame pastry?

9. Oscar: Got it! (F) <u>I know just the place.</u>

10. Green: (I) <u>Fantastic!</u> Thanks again, Oscar. (B) <u>I'm famished.</u>

　　填空之後，分作兩組，就像在機場接人一樣，一組拿著大大的名牌等著接人，另一組就是來訪的名人囉。可以用名人的名字，當然也可使用自己的名字。找到彼此之後，請進行以上這個簡短對話。練習到熟練後，請錄影存證，分享大眾。

Activity 2 Discussion

Part 1

　　你剛剛到達了一個你沒來過的國家，這時候你會想知道什麼？你會問些什麼問題？和同學討論，並寫下三個問題，同時提出可能的答案。

Part 2

　　下面這個YouTube影片裡有一位旅客剛剛到了桃園國際機場。請注意看0:33-2:20的片段就好，到底他們在問答些什麼？那位司機先生應該怎麼說比較好？

Getting out of Taipei Taoyuan Airport (by Networks from A to Z, 2014)

https://www.YouTube.com/watch?v=-Wbv9LfTAXg

如果你弄清楚在問什麼了，請看看下面的譯寫：

司機先生：In Taiwan, one? Two?

　　　　　（應該說，這是你第一次還是第二次來台灣？**Is this your first or second time in Taiwan?**）

旅　　客：First time. 第一次。

司機先生：Taiwan food?

（應該說：你期待試試看台灣食物嗎？**Are you looking forward to trying some Taiwanese food?**）

旅　　客：Yes, I think I will try. 是，我想我會試一試。

　　　　　… How long to the hotel? 10 minutes? 15 minutes? Two o'clock? One? 去旅館要多久？十分鐘？十五分鐘？兩點鐘？一點鐘？

司機先生：Yes, two.

　　　　　（應該說：我們會在兩點鐘到達旅館。大概需要半小時。**We will arrive at the hotel at two o'clock. It takes about half an hour.**）

…

旅　　客：Very hot. I like. 好熱。我喜歡。

　　　　　（旅客也開始受影響，用語變得簡單。）

司機先生：Hot. Good. 是啊，熱

　　　　　（可以說：會很熱的。夏天會超過攝氏30度，即超過華氏86度 **Yes, it can be very hot here. The temperature in the summer can be more than 30 degrees Celsius or 86 degrees Fahrenheit.**）

你覺得旅客還會問些什麼？

答：參考的問題與可能答案。

Question	Possible answers
1. How much time does it take to get to the hotel?	It will take about 50 minutes to go from the airport to the hotel in Taipei.
2. Are there any places you can recommend for me to see in Taiwan?	Most visitors like to see the National Palace Museum, which has an impressive collection of Asian treasures.

Question	Possible answers
3. How big is your organization/ school? How many employees/ students are there?	We have 500 employees. Our school has some 16,000 students.
4. How big is Taiwan? How big is the city?	以下表格的資料為可能答案，來自 Wikipedia（January, 2015）

Taiwan	In number	How to say it? 怎麼說呢
Total Area	36,193 km^2 13,974 sq mi	The total area of Taiwan is about thirty-six thousand two hundred square kilometers or about fourteen thousand square miles.
Population (Dec. 2013 estimation)	23,313,517	As of December 2013, we had about twenty three million people in our country.
Population Density	644/km^2	That is about six hundred forty people per square kilometers.

重點提示：

1. 接機禮物：接機之前，你可以在機場的旅遊服務櫃檯索取英文地圖，看你們的活動範圍在什麼地方，有城市地圖與捷運圖的最好。如果在臺北活動，你就再買一張悠遊卡當禮物，加值100-200元，這樣訪客就會覺得你好貼心。

2. 很多國外訪客在YouTube上放了自己來過台灣之後的心得分享，大家可以看看這些影片才知道別人怎麼看台灣的。只要用Taiwan當關鍵字可以找到很多這樣的影片，有的影片有字幕有的沒有，但是都只有十分鐘以內，你可以練習聽力，也可以知道來台灣的國外人士，會覺得我們的什麼東西很有趣，很不一樣。不論他們評論是好的或者讓你不開心、不舒服，其實都可以幫助我們知己知彼，幫助我們接待地更得心應手。

例如：

TRAVEL TAIWAN: THINGS you've gotta KNOW, BEFORE you GO! (by Drew's Obsessions) https://www.YouTube.com/watch?v=craHfd9n9Ys

這影片有十七個旅行台灣出發前知道的事項，包括蹲式洗手間、悠遊卡等（無字幕）

TAIWAN - The TOP 10 Most Interesting Things (by Jon Sanders)

https://www.YouTube.com/watch?v=gGxlMhde1og（有中文字幕，共有三集）

Unit 1-3 Telling Directions 如何告知搭車選項？

前言：在機場，外籍訪客遇到困難就難免會向當地人詢問路線，這個狀況常常發生，你可別躲。很多時候會有很多種解決方式，例如路線，就得慢慢說給他們聽。這單元我們看到是不認識的人問你。好好練習，以後遇到這樣的狀況，你就會回答了！

本文翻譯

（唐女士剛通過桃園國際機場海關移民署，正在問方向。）

唐女士：對不起，先生。嗨，你會說英文嗎？

雷：嗯，我會。

唐女士：哦，好！請你指引我方向好嗎？

雷：當然好，可以。

唐女士：我想從這裡到台北車站總站。不幸地，我和我司機雞同鴨講，而且我和我的聯絡人失聯了。

雷：好，我想你可以搭計程車。我可以幫您跟計程車司機說。這是最簡單的方法。

唐女士：嗯，我正想搭機場接駁車，因為我覺得一人搭計程車會感到不很舒服。

雷：我知道您的意思。那搭乘快車如何？

唐女士：這樣子很好，只要我到了台北總站，我就知道如何搭捷運。我就可以找到我住宿的旅館。這不是我第一次來台北。

雷：我可以幫您買一張車票，但是我們得先等一下我母親過海關。哦，嘿。她來了。

（雷的媽媽走近。）

雷的母親：嗨！

（雷和母親用中文說了幾句話。）

雷：我母親說您可以跟我們一起搭車。我們可以載您到飯店，因為我們也要回台北。

唐女士：哦，不用，不用。非常謝謝。請你告訴她，我不應該打擾你們。

（雷和母親再次用中文短暫交談。）

雷：她問是否您確定不用我們搭載您。我們一點都不麻煩。她問您來自何處？

唐女士：她人真好。我可以自己處理。我來自澳洲。我的父母親來自新加坡。

（雷和母親再次短暫交談。）

雷：好，那麼，如果是這樣的話，讓我帶您坐上（往台北總站的）車。

唐女士：我很感激你的幫忙。非常謝謝。

（對雷的母親說）：謝謝您。

雷：不客氣。

Activity 1 Listening practice

Part 1

以下畫線的部分就是答案。

Ms Tan: Excuse me, sir. Do you speak some ⬤ / 🇬🇧 ?

Ray: Um, yes.

Ms. Tan: Oh, good! Can you please help me with (<u>directions</u> / detections)?

Ray: Sure. I think so.

Ms. Tan: I'd like to go to 🚦 / 🚌 from here. Unfortunately, there's a mix up with my driver and I can't reach my (<u>contact</u> / connect) person.

Ray: OK. I think you can take a 🚕 / 🚌 . I can talk to the driver for you. It's the easiest way.

Ms. Tan: Um, I was thinking about riding the (<u>shuttle</u> / shuffle) bus because I'm not so comfortable with taking a taxi by myself.

Ray: I see what you mean. How about taking the express?

Ms. Tan: That could work. Once I reach Taipei Main Station, I know how to take the 🚎 / 🚆 so I should be able to find my 🏠 / 💈 . It's not my first time in Taipei.

Ray: I can help you buy a bus ticket, but we have to wait a little bit for my mother to exit (<u>customs</u> /cartoons). Oh hey. There she is.

(*Ray's mom approaches.*)

Ray's mom: Hi!

(*Ray and his mom have a short conversation in Mandarin.*)

Ray: My mom says you should (<u>ride</u> / type) with us. We can take you to your hotel since we are going back to Taipei (<u>anyway</u> / everywhere).

Ms. Tan: Oh no, no. Thank you so much. I shouldn't (<u>trouble</u> / bother) you. Please tell her that.

(*Ray and his mom have another short conversation in Mandarin.*)

Ray: She asks if you are sure. It's no trouble for us.
And... she asked where you are from.

Ms. Tan: That's very sweet of her. But I can (maintain / <u>manage</u>) on my own. And, I'm from Australia. My parents are from (<u>Singapore</u> / Switzerland).

(*Another quick conversation between mother and son.*)

Ray: OK, then. If that's the case, let me help you get (<u>on</u> / in) the right bus.

Ms. Tan: I (accustom / <u>appreciate</u>) that. Thank you so much.
(*To Ray's mom*): Hsieh hsieh ni.

Ray's mom: You're welcome.

Activity 2 Discussion

1. 為什麼唐女士拒絕雷的母親的邀請和他們一起搭車？她的理由是不是和搭計程車讓她不舒服的原因一樣？是或不是？請說明。

2. 在對話中提到唐女士有幾種方法可以到達台北車站總站？從機場到你住的城市的一間很知名的大飯店，有哪些種方法？請以英文說給你的朋友聽。

Activity 3 Understanding and applying words, idioms, and phrases

Part 1

了解下列語詞的用法，然後造出自己的句子或對話，愈幽默愈有創意愈好。

Useful expression	Application
1. Can you please help me with...? 你可以幫我…忙嗎？	• Can you help me with this heavy box? • Can you please help me with my homework?
2. There's a mix-up... （東西）搞混了…	• There was a mix-up in the schedule. • There was a mix-up over the tickets.
3. I was thinking about V-ing 我在想…	• I was thinking about getting married. • I was thinking about buying an iPhone.
4. I'm not so comfortable with Sth/ V-nig... 讓我不太自在	• I'm not so comfortable with a stranger. • I'm not so comfortable with telling lies.
5. Once S+V, S+V 事情一發生	• Once you know him, you will like him. • Once you arrive at the hotel, you need to ask them how to make international calls.
6. V... on one's own 靠自己	• I can fill in the tax return on my own.（退稅單） • Though he is only six, he can take a bus on his own.
7. If that's the case,... 假如是這樣的話	• A: It's an old car, as old as your father. B: If that's the case, I'll never ask for it. • I feel that he doesn't like me. If that's the case, I won't bother him anymore.
8. It's no trouble for us. 對我們來說不麻煩	• We'd love to do that for you. It's no trouble for us.

Useful expression	Application
	• As designers, we can help you with the interior decoration. It's no trouble for us.
9. That's very sweet of her. 她人真好。	• A: Sally said that she could be your helper in the Toastmasters. 　B: That's very sweet of her. • A: May promised to bring you some fried chicken. 　B: That's very sweet of her.
10. I appreciate that. 我很感激。	• A: We will take you to the airport. 　B: I appreciate that. • A: May promised to bring you some fried chicken. 　B: I appreciate that.

Part 2

3~4人一組，每人寫下自己家的英文地址。然後告訴同伴由家裡出發到學校所用的交通工具為何（是公車、火車、捷運、汽車或計程車）？

請用智慧型手機到下列郵局網站查詢自家的英文地址。

http://www.post.gov.tw/post/internet/Postal/index.jsp?ID=207

重點：中文地址寫法剛好跟英文相反：他們是先寫門牌號碼，接著寫「弄」，再寫「巷」，再寫「街」，再寫「市」，再寫「國家」；原則就是由小寫到大。

範例：Jessie的故事

我的名字是Jessi，我住在臺中市中華路一號。從家裡去學校一點都不麻煩，因為我家附近有公車站牌。下了公車，我還需要走十分鐘去學校。當天氣不好的時候，媽媽會開車帶我上學。好感激喔。

Chapter Two: Making Yourself at Home
賓至如歸

Unit 2-1 Solving Problems with the Netwrok
幫助解決網路問題

這個單元我們要學習怎麼照顧來訪旅客各式各樣的需求，基本態度是對方可以自己做的事情，就盡量讓他自己做，特別是當中有文化體驗的事情，就不要過度照顧，剝奪了別人的樂趣。當然，貼心還是很討人喜歡的。但要如何拿捏尺寸，須依情況而定，就請大家各自去體會了。

本文翻譯

本單元由葛林教授閱讀旅館房內的無線網路連結資訊開始。

親愛的貴客：

港灣飯店很榮幸能提供無線網路給住房客人。

連結飯店內無線網路步驟：

1. 打開無線網路卡
2. 在無線網路資訊中選取「飯店無線網路」
3. 輸入密碼：oceanside
4. 享受無線網路

若需要乙太網路，請到櫃台洽詢。

謝謝！祝您住房愉快！

誠摯的祝福

資訊支援部門

港灣飯店

（飯店房客與櫃檯人員講電話）

櫃　　檯：晚安！有可以效勞之處嗎？

葛林教授：嗨！我無法連到無線網路。我照著客人資料卡上的指示做，但是連不上線。

櫃　　檯：很抱歉，先生。可以等一下嗎？我聯絡一下看資訊工程師現在有空嗎？

葛林教授：好，沒問題。

櫃　　檯：太好了。謝謝！

…片刻後…

櫃　　檯：喂，先生。謝謝您等候。我們的資訊工程師現在有空去解決您的連結問題。方便請他在10分鐘內去您的房間嗎？

葛林教授：好。很好。謝謝您的幫忙。非常感謝。

櫃　　檯：不客氣，先生。祝您有個愉快的夜晚。

葛林教授：謝謝。也祝你愉快。

Activity 1 Listening prctice

 1.　A　 2.　H　 3.　G　 4.　D　 5.　E　 6.　F

　　　 7.　C　 8.　B

Activity 2 Discussion

1. 在台灣哪些公共區域會有免費的WiFi？（註：外籍人士可以登記使用免費的WiFi）

   Government Indoor Public Area Free WiFi System: Online Registration System for Foreign Visitors（I-Taiwan境外旅客線上登記系統）

   http://itaiwan.taiwan.net.tw/FitTravelRegister.aspx

2. 3-4人一組。首先，想想下列電訊公司的中文名字為何？其次，比較一下不同的公司有什麼不同的優缺點？

Telecom company	Chinese name
Taiwan Star Telecom	台灣之星
Asia Pacific Telecom	亞太電信
Chunghwa Telecom	中華電
VIBO Telecom	威寶電訊
Far EasTone	遠傳
Taiwan Mobile	台灣大哥大

Activity 3 Understanding and applying words, idioms, and phrases

Part 1
Practice部分的參考答案

Useful expression	Definition	Practice
1. connecting to	連接到…	• The FBI connected that man to the double cross.
2. wireless network	無線網路	• CNN, BBC, and NBC are the three major television networks.
3. be pleased to	很高興	• I'm pleased to meet you.
4. available	（在手邊）可利用的	• Jay is available to see you today.
5. Hope you have a wonderful stay with us.	希望你在我們旅館住得愉快。（短暫地住叫做stay長住在家中叫做live。）	• During the two months I stayed in the U.S., I experienced cultural shock almost every day.

Useful expression	Definition	Practice
6. have trouble + Ving	有…麻煩	• Jack has trouble fixing his car.
7. it didn't work	行不通	• We tried to get the injured man out of the car, but it didn't work.
8. the availability of	有效性、可得到的東西	• Before building the house, we must ensure the availability of man hours.
9. Thank you for holding.	謝謝你的等候。	• Hold on, please.
10. solve your connection problem	解決你的連接問題 Help you with your connection problem	• My brother can solve my computer problem.
11. I really appreciate it.	我真的很感激。	• Your help will be appreciated.
12. Same to you.	你也是一樣。	• A: Have a pleasant day. B: Thank you. Same to you.

Part 2

下列是常用的字首字母縮略詞和縮寫。

Abbreviation = 縮寫，如：Mister →Mr., Professor Lin → Prof. Lin

Acronym = 字首字母縮略詞，如：**c**ompact **d**isk → CD, **N**ational **B**asketball **A**ssociation → NBA

IT specialist	Information technology	資訊工程人員
E.E. (pronounced as "Double E")	Electrical engineer	電子工程師
CNN(I)	Cable News Network (International)	有線電視新聞網
BBC	British Broadcasting Corporation	英國廣播公司
L.A.	Los Angeles	洛杉磯

DIY	Do it yourself. 自己手作	C & P	Copy and paste 複製、貼上
LOL	Laughing out loud 大笑	2F4Y	Too fast for you 太快了
HF	Have fun 祝開心愉快	RSVP	Repondez s'il vous plait (French: Please reply) 煩請回覆
BTW	By the way 還有一事	N/A	Not available 不適用
IDK	I don't know. 不知道	OMG	Oh, my god. 我的天啦
TBA	To be announced 稍後宣告	TYT	Take your time. 慢慢來

Unit 2-2 Taking Care of You 提供醫護資訊

前言：旅行的時候最怕身體有病痛了，你招待的國外訪客可能因此狀況，求救於你。在這個單元，我們看到奧斯卡的回應，也開始想想遇到這樣的狀況，我們該怎麼幫助別人。

（葛林教授搭機來台灣後，和奧斯卡在email上連絡。）

嗨，奧斯卡：

　　很抱歉又突然來麻煩你。我剛剛不慎扭傷了背部，覺得有些不舒服。能不能麻煩你給我醫療選擇上的建議呢？假如可以，也請告訴我看醫生的花費大約多少。有了你的幫忙，我備感受到照顧。先謝謝你了。

祝福你
葛林

親愛的葛林教授：

　　希望您現在覺得好些了。明天我可以帶您去本地醫院做評估。看醫生怎麼說，我們也可以選擇看針灸醫師或按摩師。我不太確定價格會是多少，因為台灣全民健保的關係，病人只需付部分費用。不過據我所知，一般每次看醫生不會超過美金30元。針灸醫師所收的費用也差不多。
假如您有任何問題，讓我們見面再詳談吧。

祝福您！明天見！
奧斯卡

奧斯卡：

　　非常謝謝你的迅速回函。我現在比較不擔心了，我知道我在台灣看醫生的選擇了。明天見。

祝福你
葛林

Activity 1 Listening practice

Part 1

答案 1.　　A　　 2.　　E　　 3.　　C　　 4.　　D　　 5.　　B

Part 2

答案

1. local hospital
2. we also have
3. pay the full amount
4. If you have any questions
5. for the quick response

Activity 2 Discussion

1. 請討論外籍訪客可能會有怎樣的醫療需求與問題？以下是參考答案。
   - Do you happen to have Band-Aids?
     （你會不會剛好有OK繃啊？）
   - I think I have a fever. I might be coming down with something.
     （我覺得自己在發燒，可能生病了。）

- I need a foot massage.
  （想要做腳底按摩。）
- Could you introduce me to a good acupuncturist?
  （可否介紹一位很好的針灸師父？）
- How does the National Health Insurance work?
  （全民健保是怎麼一回事？）
- Is there a pharmacy around here?
  （這附近有沒有藥局？）
- Do I need a prescription for this cold medicine?
  （買這個感冒藥需不需要醫師的處方簽？）
- Where can I find a pediatrician for my daughter?
  （哪裡可以幫我女兒找到一位小兒科醫師？）

常用的專業醫師名稱

1. medical specialist 專科醫生	2. physician 內科醫生
3. surgeon 外科醫生	4. pediatrician 小兒科醫生
5. ophthalmologist 眼科醫生	6. orthopedist 骨科醫生
7. general practitioner 全科醫師	8. clinician 臨床醫師
11. dentist 牙醫	12. psychologist 心理醫生
13. therapist 治療師	14. cardiologist 心臟科醫師
15. dermatologist 皮膚科醫生	16. ENT doctor 耳鼻喉科醫生
17. allergist 過敏科醫生	18. vet (veterinarian) 獸醫
19. acupuncturist 針灸師	20. pharmacist 藥劑師

2. 假如你的背部扭傷了，你會去哪裡治療？是去看醫生、針灸師或按摩師？為什麼呢？請跟你的朋友小小辯論或討論一下：若扭傷了，看哪一種比較好？

Activity 3 Understanding and applying words, idioms, and phrases

本單元為進一步深入了解下列語詞的用法。

學會親自體驗、親自熟悉下列語詞，然後自己造句。

Useful Expression	Definition	Application
1. strained one's back	扭到了	• My grandma strained her ankle when she stood up. • My teacher strained his back when he carried a box of soaps.
2. option	選擇	• It's your option to buy or to rent. • How many options do I have?
3. If possible,...	假如可能的話… 原句為If it is possible,...	• If possible, I'll visit your family. • If possible, I'll make a cake for you.
4. in good hands	妥善得到照顧 （well taken care of 的意思）	• My mom is glad to know that her money is in good hands. • I am relieved to know that my grandma is in good hands.

Useful Expression	Definition	Application
5. in advance	事先	• I need to book train tickets in advance during New Year. • Our teacher had us prepare our food for a trip in advance.
6. Depending on...	依靠…	• Depending on how you feel, choose one of the options. • Depending on your finance, buy an affordable house.
7. Based on...	以…為基礎／基於	• Based on my knowledge, she is quite popular among young people.
8. roughly the same	大約一樣	• My twin brother's and my scores are roughly the same. • The prices of iPhone 5 and iPhone 6 are roughly the same.
9. in detail	詳細說明	• Your report should be explained in detail. • My dad does everything in detail.

Useful Expression	Definition	Application
10. in person	親自／本人	• I'll see her in person. • If you can't be there in person, you may send a gift.

Part 2

播放CD，注意聽，並用上面部分語詞與句型所組成的一篇email。說出故事的大意，並找出故事中用了以上哪些語詞，請一面聽，一面勾選。

12

媽媽給吉米的e-mail（媽媽也是吉米學校的體育組長）

親愛的吉米，

我寫這e-mail是要提醒你明天就是Browings與Childer高中的足球比賽。可能的話，是不是請把淺色與深色的球衣都帶去，這樣兩隊可以選擇他們要的顏色？我會先讓他們知道，讓他們有所準備。賽程大致上跟去年的比賽一樣。依天氣狀況而定，比賽會在體育館或戶外球場舉行。因為上周我扭傷了背，所以我沒辦法親自到比賽現場。但是，每個與賽學校會有一位監督委員到場宣告規則細節並確定一切進展順利。我跟監督委員都很熟，相信兩隊會得到最好的照顧。

順便一提，請放心，我一定會舒舒服服地在家、在我的床上好好休息。

愛你的，
媽媽

★☆★ Main idea: Jimmy's mom strained her back and is resting at home. She reminded Jimmy to do something for the football match.

How many expressions and patterns have you heard?

Answer: 10 expressions

Part 3

語言的學習很有趣，上面那篇故事用了剛學的許多語詞，你可以用幾個湊成一個或數個句子呢？試試看將兩個語詞湊成一個句子，越幽默越好！

在此推薦教育部網站（http://hsmaterial.moe.edu.tw/schema/veng/index.html）的字彙擂台賽，迸出兩個字，8秒內開口造出一個含有這兩個字的句子。

由下列12個表達語當中抽出2個，即席造句，抽完籤即刻計時30秒內，看誰造得正確又幽默。多練幾次，可以訓練你的急智喔！

Unit 2-3 Enjoying the City on Your Own
讓他自由自在趴趴走

（格蘭來自美國。他來台北參加一個商展。他和台北分公司的同事雷談話。他們很熟，所以他們之間的用字用詞很隨興。）

🎧 13

格蘭：嘿，雷。你有空嗎？

　雷：當然，什麼事？

格蘭：你知道參加這場商展，是我此行在台北的主要目的。但是我也想去看看幾個百貨公司的零售展示專櫃。

　雷：好主意，我隨時可以帶你去。

格蘭：謝謝你。那美麗華百貨公司怎麼走，我想看一下我們公司在那裡的專櫃。

雷：你是說有個大購物廣場和巨型摩天輪的地方，對嗎？你自己去那裡
　　很容易，但是我不介意這個周末帶你去那裡。

格蘭：不用了，老兄。你周末應該與家人度過。而且我這樣明天就可以自
　　　己去探索這個城市。一定很好玩。

雷：這樣的話，讓我將方向寫下來，等我幾分鐘。

格蘭：聽起來不錯。謝謝啦。

雷：不客氣。很簡單的一件事。

Activity 1 Listening practice

Grant:　Hey Ray. Do you ___(A)___ ?

Ray:　　Sure. ___(F)___ ?

Grant:　As you know, attending the trade show is my ___(E)___ in Taipei.
　　　　However, I'd like to also visit a few of the ___(C)___ that are in the
　　　　department stores.

Ray:　　Ah, that's a great idea. I can take you ___(B)___ .

Grant:　___(D)___ . I want to ask you for directions to Miramar (美麗華). We
　　　　have a counter there.

．．．

Ray:　　You mean the shopping center with the giant ___(J)___ , right? It's
　　　　easy to get there, but I ___(M)___ taking you this weekend.

Grant:　___(H)___ . You should spend the weekend with your family. Besides,
　　　　I can ___(G)___ by myself tomorrow. ___(N)___ .

Ray:　　In that case, let me ___(I)___ the directions for you. Give me ___(K)___ .

Grant:　Sounds good. Thanks a lot.

Ray:　　You're welcome. ___(L)___ .

Activity 2 Discussion

Part 1

1. 從哪些隨性的對話中可以看出雷和格蘭兩人是熟友？

   Do you have a minute? What's up? No, man.

   常用口語用法語詞：

   Hit the road. 上路

   I'm running late. 我快遲到了。

   Hang out. 和朋友在一起。

   I think we two really click. 我倆合得來。

   That sucks. 真遜！

   Dump my boyfriend/girlfriend. 甩掉男（女）朋友。

2. 假如你是格蘭，你比較喜歡雷帶你逛這個城市或者獨自探險？

3. 其實大部份的人可能比較喜歡自己自由自在地探索一個城市。身為國外訪客的在台友人，你覺得他們會需要什麼東西或建議，幫助他們享受這個城市同時也保持安全呢？

Part 2

兩人一組，演出本文內容，內容可以大致相同，但記得你接受或反對的理由要和本文不同，也可以提供意見與物件，幫助旅人享受這個城市。

Activity 3 Understanding and applying words, idioms, and phrases

Part 1

了解下列片語和句子的意思，接著和同學討論在何種情況下，會常使用到這些句子。

兩人一組製造出一些有趣的對話。

1. Do you have a minute?	你有時間嗎？（你有空嗎？）
2. What's up? (What's the matter?) (What can I do for you?) (Can I do something for you?)	什麼事？
3. Thanks for the offer. Thank you for your help.	謝謝你願意幫助。
4. You mean... (Do you mean...?)	你的意思是…
5. I really don't mind taking you this weekend.	這周末我真的不介意帶你去。
6. No, man.	不用，老兄。
7. Let me write up the direction for you.	我寫下地址／方向給你。
8. In that case,…	在這情況之下…（要是這樣的話…）
9. Give me a couple of minutes.	給我幾分鐘的時間。
10. Sounds good.	聽起來不錯。
11. It's a piece of cake. (It's easy.) (It's as easy as ABC.) (It's as easy as pie.) (It's really simple.) (It's no big deal.) (It's no sweat at all.) (It's a cinch.) (It's a no-brainer.)	這很簡單。

Part 2

 15

(A)

Bruce: Sorry, Nancy, I can't attend the meeting around 9 because I need to drop some papers at Sogo University around 10.

Nancy: In that case, let's change the time. How about 10:30?

Bruce: Sure. That will be great!

 16

(B)

Sally: Hi, Johnny. Do you have a minute?

Johnny: Sure. What's up?

Sally: I will buy a motorbike. Are you free to go with me this afternoon?

Johnny: Cool! I'd love to.

Sally: Thank you for your offer.

Johnny: You are very welcome.

Chapter Three: Arriving at the Conference
會場報到

Unit 3-1 Checking in at the Conference
會場報到會說什麼？

前言：很多來台灣的外籍訪客，是因為工商展覽或者是研討會而來。這個單元我們就跟他們去研討會看看，會發生什麼事情。如果你有機會在研討會場服務，希望你在外籍訪客眼中會是個很能幹的工作人員！

本文翻譯

丹尼斯：哈囉。歡迎光臨研討會。請問貴姓？

大衛士：嗨，是的，我的名字叫珍·大衛士。

丹尼斯：請等一下。讓我看一下。啊，在這裡。大衛士教授，高興和您見面。這是您的名牌和您的餐券。

大衛士：謝謝你。我要素食餐點，是否可以幫我確認一下？

丹尼斯：當然，這張餐券是綠色的，表示我們會提供您素食午餐和飲料。

大衛士：太好了。

丹尼斯：同時，這裡有一個大會提供的提袋，內有會議議程和贊助者的促銷物品。

大衛士：太棒了！正是我所需要的。很快的問一個問題：下一場主題演講在哪裡？什麼時候？

丹尼斯：下一場主題演講大約五分鐘後在大廳開始，大廳在您的右手邊的電梯旁。

大衛士：喔，很好，我還有幾分鐘時間。

丹尼斯：假如您有問題或需要協助，我們都會隨時在此提供協助。

大衛士：好。我注意到服務人員都穿著亮色背心。

丹尼斯：是的，很難不看到我們。我們很亮（雙關語：也有很聰明的意思）。

大衛士：確實，謝謝你們的幫忙。

丹尼斯：不客氣，大衛士教授。祝您愉快。

1 Listening practice

答案

Dennis: Hello. Welcome to the conference. May I have your (<u>name</u> / phone number / age), please?

Davis: Hi. Yes, my name is Jane Davis.

Dennis: Just a (minute / <u>moment</u> / second), please. Let me take a look. Ah, here it is. It's nice to meet you Professor Davis. Here is your name (back / pack / <u>badge</u>) and your meal voucher.

Davis: Thank you. I (stayed/ <u>requested</u> /asked) a vegetarian meal so can you please (<u>verify</u> / vary / carry) that for me?

Dennis: Certainly. This voucher is (<u>green</u> / free / tree), which means that you will be provided a vegetarian lunch and (soda / <u>beverage</u> / drink).

Davis: Great.

Dennis: Also, here's a complimentary tote bag that contains a conference agenda, a floor plan, as well as some (<u>promotional items</u> / additional ideas) from our sponsors.

Davis: Wonderful. This is exactly what I need. Just a very (clear / <u>quick</u> / small) question: where and when is the next keynote speech?

Dennis: The next keynote speech starts (at / on / <u>in</u>) about five minutes at the main hall, which is next to the elevator on your (ride / <u>right</u> / side).

Davis: Oh good. I have a few more minutes.

Dennis: If you have any (station / problems / <u>questions</u>) or need any help, all of us are here to assist.

Davis: Fantastic. I noticed that the staff members are wearing (<u>bright</u> / tight / white) colored vests.

Dennis: Yes, hard to (cross / <u>miss</u> / pass). We are very bright.

Davis: Indeed. Thank you very much for your help.

Dennis: You're welcome, Professor Davis. Have a good time.

Activity 2 Discussion

1. 你曾經參加過任何會議嗎？會議的內容是什麼？請跟朋友聊這方面的經驗。

2. 名牌上一般都會寫些什麼？
   （參考會議名牌製作網站，請用conference name badge當關鍵字查詢Google image.）

3. 最近一次您登記進入某個地方是何時？在何處登記？飯店、會議或機場？

Activity 3 Understanding and applying words, idioms, and phrases

Part 1

在這篇對話中，出現了許多會議或研討會比較常出現的東西，比如說姓名牌或餐券。讓我們一起來學學如何用英文表達這些實用的東西吧！

name badge	姓名牌
meal voucher	餐券
vegetarian meal	素食餐
complimentary tote bag	贈送隨身包
conference agenda	會議議程
floor plan	樓層平面圖
promotional items	促銷產品
keynote speech	主題報告；專題演講

Part 2

除了上述的實用名詞，會議接待人員Denise的說話內容還包括一些比較禮貌的用詞喔！當我們和他人對話想試著禮貌些，不妨說說看這些句子吧！

> May I have your name, please? 請問貴姓大名？
> Just a moment, please. 請稍等一下。
> Here is your ... 這是你的…
> If you have any questions or need any help, all of us are here to assist. 如果有任何問題，我們都會為您服務。
> Have a good time. 祝你愉快。

Part 3

戲劇時間：

學了上面的用詞及句子，請兩兩一組，每組自行編寫一段約三分鐘的對話，對話內容至少要用到3個學到的物品或句子喔！編好後花5-10分鐘練習，並請不同組同學輪流上台，將對話演出來給班上同學看。

Unit 3-2 Responding to Requests 如何回應相關需求？

本文翻譯

格　　　蘭：對不起，在我的出席會議資料袋中，沒有主題演說的議程表。你有多的議程表嗎？

工作人員1：對不起。請再說一次。

格　　　蘭：好，當然。請你給我一張主題演說的議程表好嗎？我的提袋中沒有這張表。

工作人員1：喔，好的。我知道了。

（遞給格蘭另外一個全新的含所有資料的提袋）

格　　　蘭：喔，不用。我只需要主題演說的議程表就好了。

工作人員1：嗯，對不起，請等一下。

格　　　蘭：好的。慢慢來。

工作人員2：嗨，有可以效勞之處嗎？

格　　蘭：哈囉，是的。我沒有拿到主題演說的議程表。你有多的嗎？

工作人員2：啊，當然有。對不起有點亂。我馬上拿一張給您。

格　　蘭：沒關係。不用感到抱歉。非常謝謝你們兩位。

Activity 1 Listening practice

Part 1
仔細聽聽CD內容，在空格中填入代號。

(1) A (a list of keynote speakers)

(2) C (a copy of)

(3) G (complimentary tote bag)

(4) D (wait a moment)

(5) H (Take your time)

(6) E (extra)

(7) F (any confusion)

(8) B (apologize)

Part 2
再次聽CD，並選出正確的答案。

錄音稿：

Question 1: What did Grant ask for?

Question 2: What did the first staff member give Grant?

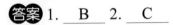 1.　B　　2.　C

Activity 2 Discussion

1. 你有沒有過這樣的經驗，外籍訪客在你沒預期的狀況下問了你一個問題？請跟同學聊一下這樣的經驗，當時你有什麼樣的感覺？

2. 全球化的現在，隨時可能有機會考驗自己的英文能力。請問有什麼方法可以增加自己臨時回應英文問題的能力？（建議：多閱讀英文的書報雜誌，儘量爭取說話的機會，自己一人也可以假想與人對談討論這些議題。）

3. 另一方面，很多國際訪客來台灣是因為想學中文。你有沒有想過如果他們想學英文，但是我們卻一直堅持用英文回應他們，他們會怎麼想？會不會覺得不受歡迎，不受鼓勵？（註：其實很多外國人很不喜歡我們換成英文跟他們說話喔，因為似乎是暗示他說得不夠好，像是在跟他說你乾脆不要試了，反正你學不會！我們的一片好心換成說英文，其實卻很傷人呢！）

4. 如果你知道外籍訪客來台是因為要學中文，但又不能了解你說的中文，你可以怎麼幫他？但是只可以用中文，不用英文喔（註：其實只要多說幾次他就會知道了！最好是用同樣的文字，不要每次都換不同的字，初學者是沒辦法接招的。）

Activity 3 Understanding and applying words, idioms, and phrases

Part 1
學一些有用的語詞，利用手機查一下網路，並將答案填入空格內。

Useful expression	Definition	Application
1. a list of	列單	I need a list of groceries for tonight's dinner party.
2. keynote speaker	主題演說家	Being a keynote speaker is not easy.
3. attendee	出席的人	All those attendees were fashion designers.
4. a copy of (the book or conference agenda)	一本書 一張（議程）	I need you to run to 7-11 to make a copy of my ID card.

Useful expression	Definition	Application
5. contain	包含	The schoolbag contains some school supplies（即文具）and books.
6. apologize	道歉	Grace apologized to me for being late for the meeting.

Part 2

如果你會用以下的說法，別人就會覺得你是個有禮貌的年輕人哦！

試著跟同學討論下面這些句子在哪些情況下會用到：

1. Can you please say that again?
2. Please wait a moment.
3. Take your time.
4. How can I help you?
5. Sorry for any confusion.
6. Don't apologize.

Part 3

兩人一組，閱讀下面對話並試著在Part 2中的6個句子裡找出最適合的答案。找出所有答案後請選一組對話，將它延伸成一分鐘的小短劇，然後一起表演給班上同學看喔！

Question 1:

A: Let me find it for you.

B: Take your time.

Question 2:

A: Sorry for any confusion.

B: It's fine. No need to worry.

Question 3:

A: Sorry for making the mistake.

B: Don't apologize.

Question 4:

A: How can I help you?

B: Oh, I have some problem with the computer.

Question 5:

A: I want a cup of tea, please.

B: I can't hear you. Can you please say that again?

Question 6:

A: Is your boss here? I would like to see him.

B: Sure. Please wait a moment.

Chapter Four: Attending the Conference
參加會議

Unit 4-1 **Welcoming Remarks** 如何代表大會致歡迎詞？

〔會議廳內，莎拉楊拿著麥克風對觀眾說話〕

莎拉（說話中）：

　　親愛的同事們，早安！很高興看到諸位。歡迎您來到年會的第一天。我的名字是莎拉・楊，行銷部副總。

　　我們即將展開令人興奮的一天。開始前，我要提醒大家將各位的手機轉為靜音模式。謝謝。

　　在您的手中應該有今天的議程。今天早上我們的執行長、貴賓和我，將會說明Acme公司的下一個會計年度的行銷目標。午餐後，您將加入自己的團隊開會。今天活動結束前大家將在員工交誼廳相見歡。

　　我們的公司的夥伴一直很認真地在主辦這次會議。我們希望這次的會議將是一次令您滿意且愉快的經驗。現在讓我們歡迎我們的執行長摩根・李。

議程表

第一天		主持人
09:00-09:15	歡迎會	莎拉・楊（Acme公司行銷副總）
09:15-10:15	主題演講	摩根・李（Acme公司執行長）
		漢克・葛林教授（ABC大學教授）
10:15-10:30	中場休息	
10:30-12:00	主題演講（續）	
	發問時間	
12:00-1:30	午餐	

第一天	主持人
1:30-3:00	商業單位群組 會議
3:00-5:00	歡迎茶會

 1 Listening practice

Part 1

注意聽CD並將所聽到的字圈起來。

答案 以下畫線者為答案。

Sarah (speaking):

Dear Colleagues, good morning! It's really (<u>wonderful</u> / beautiful) to see everyone. Let me welcome you to the first day of our (monthly /<u>annual</u>) meeting. My name is Sarah Yang, VP (Vice President) of marketing and sales.

We have an exciting day (<u>ahead of</u> / in front of) us, but before we begin, I'd like to (tell / <u>remind</u>) everyone to please switch your mobile phones to silent-mode. Thank you.

In your hands, you should have the (<u>agenda</u> / activity) for today. For the majority of the morning, our CEO, a special guest and I will lead you through Acme's marketing goals for the next fiscal year. After lunch, you will join your team for (<u>group meetings</u> / tea break). We will end this day with a happy hour in our employee lounge.

Our staff has done a great job organizing this conference. We hope you will find it (an interesting / <u>a fulfilling</u>) and enjoyable experience. With that, please welcome our CEO, Mr. Morgan Lee.

Part 2

仔細聽下面播放的 CD，再依問題選出答案。每個片段請重複聽兩次。

CD片段一：

We have an exciting day ahead of us, but before we begin, I'd like to remind everyone to please switch your mobile phones to silent mode. Thank you.

CD片段二：

Our staff has done a great job organizing this conference. We hope you will find it a fulfilling and enjoyable experience. With that, please welcome our CEO, Mr. Morgan Lee.

答案 1. ___B___ 2. ___C___

Activity 2 Discussion

兩兩一組，和同學聊聊這些問題。

1. 請跟同伴分析一下莎拉的演講稿。她是怎麼開始的？給了什麼資訊？她是怎麼結束的？這簡短的演講目的何在？接著，請準備一個類似的演說稿，可能是某個場合要用的，練習好後請在班上說，或者說給你的朋友聽。

2. 上回你聽到手機在不適當的時間點響了起來，是什麼時候？是你的手機嗎？手機在不該響起時響了起來，你有什麼感覺？請跟你的朋友聊聊這樣的經驗。

Activity 3 Understanding and applying words, idioms, and phrases

Part 1

除了靜音模式，手機裡還有什麼模式呢？拿起手機來跟partner比較一下吧！你的手機有以下這些模式嗎？請與你的朋友聊聊這些模式都是在什麼時候使用呢？

FLIGHT/ AIRPLANE MODE 飛航模式	NORMAL MODE 正常模式	OUTDOOR MODE 戶外模式	MEETING MODE 會議模式	DRIVING MODE 駕駛模式	SILENT MODE 靜音模式

Part 2

看著下面圖片，找一位同學一起練習下列的表達語詞，並試著寫下屬於你自己的句子吧！

參考答案

1. Let me welcome you to Taipei 101.
2. I like to remind everyone not to smoke in the meeting room.
3. In your hands, you should have a bunch of flowers.
4. We will end this day with a tea party.

Unit 4-2 Introducing the Presenter 怎麼介紹主講人？

前言：這一篇是介紹主講人。通常會提供對方的重點資歷與背景，也會有些小小幽默，緩和一下緊張的氣氛。大家可以去研討會場體驗看看，就知道這個場合通常滿正式的。有機會擔任介紹人的角色，可是很大的榮耀噢！

（執行長致詞）

謝謝，莎拉。

早安，同事們。歡迎來到台北。這裡有好幾位經過長途跋涉而來，我也在此表達謝意。

過去幾年，Acme公司在大家的努力下創造出優秀的產品，提供亮眼的服務，達成公司的持續經營與成長。希望未來我們能秉持同樣的承諾，繼續創造卓越。

為了更加強企業經營，從去年年底，我們便與ABC大學合作。由莎拉帶領的團隊與葛林教授一直都在設法改進我們的行銷策略與執行方法。身為大學教授與行銷系主任，葛林教授有超過30年的教學、研究經驗，也與亞洲多國企業有合作。我們真是從葛林教授處受益良多。今天早上我們三人要跟大家分享我們的合作成果，以及公司經營如何因此而有所修正。之後的開放討論時間，希望能得到大家的回饋。好，那我們就別再耽誤了，請一起來歡迎葛林教授。

Activity 1 Listening practice

24

Part 1

注意聽CD，然後回答問題。

Professor Tom Cruise is the chairman of the production department, with over 30 years of teaching, research and collaboration with Silicon Valley companies. For the past year, we have been working on the integration of academic research and our production goals. This morning, he and I will share the results of our partnership with you.

At the end of this morning's session, we'd like to open up the floor for Q & A. A copy of the presentation is available on our server, so you don't have to worry about writing everything down.

答案 1. ___D___ 2. ___C___ 3. ___B___ 4. ___A___

 25

Part 2

注意聽CD，然後填入適當的答案。

To build a better business, we <u>entered</u> into a partnership with the University of ABC at the end of last year. Sarah's <u>team</u> has been working with Professor James Green to <u>improve</u> our marketing strategies and execution. As a faculty member and current dean of the marketing department, Professor Green has over <u>25 years of</u> experience in teaching, research and collaboration with multi-national companies <u>in</u> Asia. This morning, the <u>two</u> of us will share the results of our work with you and how they will shape our approach.

答案 畫線部分為答案

Activity 2 Discussion

1. 在會議中當一位主席需要很多的技巧。跟你的夥伴討論一下，並列出一張單子，對於主持會議時開頭應該說些什麼？然後和夥伴們多練習幾次。

   例如：開場白不能太長，簡短幾句就好，如：稱呼、自我短暫介紹、問候、天氣、到會議室的旅途、感謝蒞臨、會議地簡介等等。介紹時要幽默，使與會者放鬆心情，面帶微笑等。

2. 在台灣何處可以練習作為一位優秀英語講者？

   參考答案：我們在此推薦國際演講協會The Toastmasters Club。國際演講協會總部在美國，是一個歷史悠久的非營利機構，旨在幫助會員訓練語言能力、人際關係和領導才能。在台灣他們叫做中華民國國際演講協會，已經有四十年以上的歷史了。在台灣一共有五種語言的俱樂部：英語、國語、日語、客家語和閩南語。各地都有他們的分會，你可以在住家或者工作單位附近找到Toastmasters。（http://www.toastmasters.org.tw/）各地分會列表：http://seo.docs.com.tw/blue/register.php?search=english&page_type=list&status=done#records 小編大推！

Activity 3 Understanding and applying words, idioms, and phrases

Part 1

學會下列的表達，然後利用這些表達方式自己造句。

Sentences for your reference:

- All my colleagues are young men.
- BigByte is an exceptional language school.
- Good students can sustain their commitment to hand in their papers on time.
- My teacher makes a commitment to give us fried chicken if all of us pass the final test.
- We are seeking a business partnership in hi-tech development.
- Teaching strategies are quite important in teaching lower-achievers.
- The execution of the killer will take place in a few days.
- The dean of our Applied English Department is a sweet lady.
- Collaboration with ASUS makes all the colleagues excited.

Part 2

練習當主持人的演說詞。然後不看稿演說。務必自然地加上一些肢體動作。

Unit 4-3 Keynote Speech 主題演講：聽演講記筆記

本文翻譯

以下是葛林教授在研討會發表演說中的一小部份內容：

謝謝摩根先生的介紹。真高興有人給我這種規格的注目。

　　首先，我要恭喜上年度你們的計畫都非常成功。這個行業競爭很激烈，但是Acme公司成功地在這樣激烈的競爭中保持領先的地位。跟莎拉以及Acme團隊一起工作之後，我們回到了最根本的問題：市場的需求是什麼？因此，我們重新開始檢視我們的行銷策略，並在幾個重要的面向蒐集了寶貴的資料，比如說目標市場、競爭者的表現、以及目前和未來的市場環境。重要的是，行銷研究幫助我們決定是否要調整，或者如何來分配我們的資源。

　　我知道這些都是比較廣泛的概念，所以在摩根和莎拉的幫忙之下，我們將要開始討論細節。最後，我也邀請你們大家一起來做評論，並提出問題。當然，如果你覺得不好意思提或者沒有時間提，可以把意見email給我。重點是你們的回饋對我們而言都是非常寶貴的。

Activity 1 Listening practice

Part 1

請根據CD選擇適合的填空。

1. The competition in this industry is fierce, but Acme has managed to _____
   __(A)__ .
   (A) stay ahead of the game
   (B) stay above troubles
   (C) steadily win the game
   (D) steadily generate profits

2. In essence, marketing research helps us determine whether to make adjustments and how to ____ (C) ____ .
   (A) collect our resources
   (B) manage our resources
   (C) allocate our resources
   (D) accept our resources

3. With the help of Morgan and Sarah, we will begin our discussion with
   ____ (C) ____ .

(A) general

(B) generalization

(C) specifics

(D) specifications

4. Of course, you may email them to us if you are shy or if we ___(B)___ .

(A) run out of money

(B) run out of time

(C) run out of cash

(D) run out of resources

5. The point is that your input is extremely ___(D)___ to us.

(A) expensive

(B) important

(C) manageable

(D) valuable

Part 2

上面的演說只是一個簡單的示範。我們鼓勵你聽TED的演講。下面我們選擇比較完整的演講，都跟學習有關。聽的時候，請你寫筆記或畫個觀念圖，標示出這些演講到底是如何組織的。

Activity 2 Discussion

以上的演說都是有關效率學習的方法。你覺得學習得可以這麼快、這麼有效率嗎？你自己的語言學習經驗是什麼樣的狀況呢？請用三到五分鐘以演講模式說明你對以上演說的心得感想。

Unit 4-4 Q & A 演講後的提問與討論＋怎麼提問才能聊得起來？

本文翻譯

莎拉：現在，讓我們開放發問。

史黛西：哈囉，葛林教授，不好意思，我英文不好。我可以問您一個問題嗎？

葛林教授：當然！這就是我們在這裡的目的。請問大名？

史黛西：不好意思，我的名字叫做史黛西。

葛林教授：哈囉，史黛西。首先，你的英文不錯。但是更重要的是，你有勇氣在這麼多人面前說話，就應該給自己鼓勵。所以，你的問題是什麼？

史黛西：謝謝教授。先前您提到跟市場契合的重要性。請您再多解釋一下這個觀念，好嗎？謝謝。

葛林教授：好問題！我很高興能詳細解說。這個觀念很簡單但是很重要：公司應該要了解顧客的需求。當然，這需要專注投入大量人力與財力資源。

摩根：說得好，教授。坦白地說，有時我們會對產品過度有信心。所以，提醒自己要常常跟顧客與一般市場連繫是很重要的。厲害的公司甚至會事先預期市場需要。這是我們的目標。

葛林教授：史黛西，我希望我們已經回答了你的問題。

摩根：如葛林教授先前所提的，我們鼓勵你們提供回饋和提出問題。Acme是我們的公司，所以我們都得努力達成成功。

Activity 1 Listening practice

Part 1

聽CD填入正確的答案

Professor Lee: So far we have talked about stock market. Any question?

Student Ma: Sorry for my Chinese English. May I ask you a question?

Professor Lee: Sure! Go ahead!

Student Ma: What's the difference between bear market and bull Market?

Professor Lee: Bear market is a special term for the stock market being in a down trend, or a period of falling stock prices. This is the opposite of a bull market. Bull market is when the stock market is in a period of increasing stock prices.

Part 2

請根據CD選擇適合的填空。

That's a good point, Professor. Frankly, <u>at times</u>, we are <u>overly</u> confident about our products. So, it's important to <u>remind</u> ourselves to be more <u>in touch with</u> the customer base and the market <u>in general</u>. Great companies are even able to <u>anticipate</u> market demand. That's our goal.

Activity 2 Discussion

Part 1

很多同學都不太會問問題,也就是說問問題本身就是個大問題。在這個活動裡,你有很多機會問問題,而且你也只能用問題來當作回答。如果你用直述句回應,那就輸了。我們來看看,你跟你的學伴可以持續這樣問問題問多久。下面是個例子,先做個示範來開始:

A: Do you want to go to a movie?
　　想去看電影嗎?

B: What movie?
　　什麼電影?

A: Don't you remember how I told you about the movie 'Joy'?
　　你記得我跟你提過翻轉幸福這部電影嗎?

B: What about it? 這電影怎麼樣?

A: Have you ever thought about inventing something like a powerful mop?
　　你有沒有想過發明一個很厲害的拖把?

B: What!? Who would invent such a stupid thing?
　　蝦米!怎麼會有人發明這樣的東西啊?

A:　... (*continue...*)(請繼續)

Part 2

請跟同伴討論:跟訪客閒聊的時候,要怎麼問問題才能夠雙方都聊得很熱烈、很開心。

建議：好問題通常是可以有很多面向思考的問題，而且參與討論的人也必須有能力提供不同方向的思考。要讓所有人都能開心參與，就要多關心別人，想想參與人知道什麼、關心什麼，讓他們可以不必費心準備，馬上就可以參與討論。

以下這個網站有相當不錯的資訊，建議大家好好研究一下，隨時準備好幾個題目：How to come up with Good Conversation topics (with sample topics) by Wikihow http://www.wikihow.com/Come-Up-with-Good-Conversation-Topics

這網站裡共有三部分的資訊，非常多建議話題。這裡把比較容易入手的話題放在這裡，方便大家學習：

1. 一般人不太喜歡聊宗教信仰、政治、賺多少錢等等攸關私人的事情，一定要注意避免。

2. 問對方的興趣嗜好：文中舉出的問題例子包括：

   • Do you play or follow any sports? 你喜歡做什麼運動或追蹤何種運動賽事？

   • Do you like to hang out online? 你喜歡在網路上做些什麼？

   • What do you like to read? 你都讀什麼書？

   • What do you do in your spare time? 空閒的時間你都做些什麼？

   • What kind of music do you like? 你喜歡聽什麼樣的音樂？

   • What kinds of movies do you like to watch? 你喜歡看什麼樣的電影？

   • What are your favorite TV shows? 你最喜歡的電視節目是什麼？

   • What's your favorite board game or card game? 你最喜歡什麼桌遊？

   • Do you like animals? What's your favorite animal? 你喜歡動物嗎？最喜歡的動物是什麼？

3. 談談家人，文中說：問對方的兄弟姐妹比較安全，若問婚姻、小孩、父母都有可能惹人不開心。如果對方願意說，那就沒問題，建議大家回應得熱情些，可以鼓勵對方多說一點。建議的問題包括：

   • Do you have any siblings? How many? 你有兄弟姐妹嗎？幾位呢？

   • (If he/she has no siblings) What was it like being an only child?（如果沒有兄弟姐妹）當個獨生女／子是什麼樣的感覺？

- (If he/she has siblings) What are their names?（若有兄弟姐妹）他們叫什麼名字？
- What do your siblings do? (Modify the question based on how old they are. Do they go to school/college or have a job?) 你的兄弟姐妹現在在做什麼？
- Do you look alike? 你跟你兄弟姐妹長得像不像？
- Do you all have similar personalities? 你們的個性像不像？
- Where did you grow up? 你們是在哪裡長大的？

4. 問對方的旅遊經驗或者想去哪裡旅行。

   建議的問題：

   - If you had a chance to move to any other country, which one would it be and why?
     如果你有機會搬到別的國家，你最想搬去哪裡？為什麼？
   - Of all the cities in the world you've visited, which one was your favorite?
     你去過世界上這麼多城市，哪一個你最喜歡？
   - Where did you go on your last vacation? How did you like it?
     你上次度假去哪裡？喜不喜歡那裡呢？
   - What was the best/worst vacation or trip you've ever been on?
     你覺得自己經歷過最好或是最糟糕的旅行是去哪裡？

5. 可以問關於食物的問題，但是要小心，別討論烈酒，也別讓討論進入減肥的問題，免得踢到鐵板。

   建議的問題：

   - If you could only have one meal for the rest of your life, what would it be?
     如果這是你這一生的最後一餐，你想吃什麼？
   - Where do you like to go when you eat out?
     你外食的時候都選什麼樣的地方吃？
   - Do you like to cook?
     你喜歡自己煮飯菜嗎？

- What's your favorite kind of candy or dessert?
  你最喜歡的甜食是什麼？

- What's the worst restaurant experience you've ever had?
  你有沒有遭遇過很糟糕的用餐經驗？

6. 問對方所從事的工作，也不錯，要小心不要變成好像在面試一樣。保持短而有趣的原則就好。（千萬別問別人賺多少錢！）

- What do you do for a living? Where do you work (or study)?
  你從事哪一行？在哪裡服務？

- What was your first job ever?
  你的第一份工作是什麼？

- Who was your favorite boss in the past?
  你最喜歡的老闆是誰？

- When you were a kid, what did you want to be when you grew up?
  你小時候希望長大後做什麼？

- What do you like best about your job?
  你最喜歡自己工作的哪個部分？

- If money was no object, but you still had to work, what would be your dream job?
  如果不用考慮錢，你最想要的夢幻工作是什麼？

7. 最好的辦法是給別人由衷的讚美，但是別說別人的眼睛好美、身體好壯！跟身體特徵相關的問題，真的很不合適，別人會接不下話的，而且不知道你想做什麼（不懷好意嗎？）。

建議題目：

- I loved your piano performance. How long have you been playing?
  好喜歡你剛才的鋼琴表演。請問你從事這樣的演出多久了？

- You made many important points during your speech. Could you elaborate on _____？
  你剛剛演講的時候談到好幾個重點。可否多討論一下某一個點？（類似我們這個單元裡史黛西問的問題。）

Chapter Five: Going Out After the Conference
會後出遊

Unit 5-1 Going Out and Enjoying Ourselves 訂出遊計劃

本文翻譯

艾倫：嘿，凱倫！

凱倫：嗨，艾倫！

艾倫：人生第一次，在年會中，我真正享受種種不同的討論和演講。我這樣說好像很怪，但我真覺得自己正身處一個很偉大的事件當中。

凱倫：我也有這種想法！自從我進公司後，我覺得我的努力真的能改善些什麼。

艾倫：知道自己的努力受到重視，而且有機會進步成長，這種感覺真好。

凱倫：非常同意！好，不談工作了。我們一大票同事要去永康街吃吃喝喝。你要跟我們去嗎？

艾倫：好哇，我想去。即使這幾天的會議既有意議又有趣，我也想出去透透氣。所以計畫是什麼？

凱倫：當然是鼎泰豐小龍包囉！之後，我還要設法變出肚子空間繼續吃麻辣牛肉麵。至於喝些什麼，還沒有決定。

艾倫：聽起來很棒啊。我知道有一間小酒吧可容納下一大夥人。

凱倫：好啊。

艾倫：你們什麼時候要出去？

凱倫：我們有部分人要先回旅館梳洗一番，30分鐘後就能準備好出發。

艾倫：好。所以，7:30在東門捷運站見面？

凱倫：太好了！我知道怎麼去那兒。等下見了。

艾倫：拜拜。

Activity 1 Listening practice

Part 1 (答案是下面有劃線的部分)

Aaron: Hey Karen!

Karen: Hi Aaron.

Aaron: For once in my life, I really (<u>enjoyed</u> / joined) the various talks and presentations in this annual meeting. This sounds strange, but I feel that I'm part of something big.

Karen: I have the same (ideas / <u>thoughts</u>) too! Ever since I joined this company, I feel that my efforts actually make a difference.

Aaron: It's a good feeling to know that we are (agreed / <u>appreciated</u>) and we have the opportunity to learn and grow.

Karen: I can't agree more!

Now, enough about work. A bunch of us from the office are going to Yong Kang Street for some food and (<u>drinks</u> / food).

Do you want to join us?

Aaron: Yeah, I would love to. Even though the meetings in the last few days were meaningful and interesting, I could really take a (<u>break</u> / vacation) too. So what's the plan?

Karen: Dumplings at Ding Tai Feng, of course! After that, I'll need to *miraculously* make room for some spicy (chicken / <u>beef</u>) noodles. As for drinks, we're not sure yet.

Aaron: Oh man. That sounds wonderful. I know a small bar that's good for a big group.

Karen: Good.

Aaron: When are you guys heading out?

Karen: A few of us are heading back to the hotel to (<u>freshen</u> / clean) up so we'll be ready in about 30 minutes.

Aaron: Okay. So, let's meet at 7:30 at Dongmen Station?

Karen: Perfect! I know (perfectly / <u>exactly</u>) how to get there. See you soon.

Aaron: Bye for now.

Part 2

 31

Aaron: When are you guys heading out?

Karen: A few of us are heading back to the hotel to freshen up so we'll be ready in about 30 minutes.

Aaron: Okay. So, let's meet at 7:30 at Dongmen Station?

Karen: Perfect! I know exactly how to get there. See you soon.

Aaron: Bye for now.

Question 1: Where are they going to meet?

   B

 32

Karen: As for drinks, we're not sure yet.

Aaron: Oh, man. That sounds wonderful. I know a small bar that's good for a big group.

Karen: Good.

Question 2: What is the place they are more likely to go after eating?

   C

Activity 2 Discussion

外籍友人第一次來台灣開會，會後你會帶他去哪裡玩呢？請跟你的朋友商量並設計一個半天、一天或兩天的行程。設計之前，請想想對方的背景：比方他的年齡、喜好與職業。然後，你要說服觀眾你的設計是最好的（可能是最好玩，但是又最經濟）。

建議：第一就先參考觀光局的資訊：http://eng.taiwan.net.tw/

但是 →

因為台灣人都帶外籍訪客吃小籠包，都送他們鳳梨酥，最近已經有些常來台灣的訪客或者在台灣有很多親友的，都說有點膩了，可不可以換點別的。另外，也有不想花大錢的，或想體驗台灣人真實生活的（而非觀光客才會去看或去做的事情）。遇到這樣的訪客，就要量身打造有特色的，其實我們生活四周都可能帶他們去體驗。例如可以逛傳統市場（traditional markets），小村莊（villages）、節慶活動（festivals）、藝術表演（art performances）、騎單車逛市區（tour the city by U-bikes, iBike, C-Bike 等）、傳統茶店喝茶買茶（tea houses）、腳底按摩（receive a food massage）、體驗台灣的婚紗攝影（wedding photo studios）等等，都會讓國外訪客覺得花錢不多，但大有趣味。

有故事的地方都很有趣味。例如，台灣的便利商店密度極高，也與全球其他各地的便利商店不同，非常值得逛逛。歐美人仕初來到台灣會找星巴克買咖啡，你可以建議他試試便利商店的咖啡，通常會覺得居然跟他們的便利商店賣的低品質咖啡不同。好玩的是7-11還有故事噢，你知道7-11怎麼變成24小時營業的嗎？其實是個美麗的錯誤，有天晚上鐵捲門壞了7-11只好不關門，老闆與老闆娘留守，沒想到當晚客人絡繹不絕，於是發現原來晚上消費者的需求很高，慢慢形成了24小時營業狀態請見：台灣小確幸(1)便利商店全球最強 - Taiwan Convenience Stores Are The Best https://www.YouTube.com/watch?v=jMRc8W6jYBk

所以建議大家多考慮帶訪客去有故事的地方，例如一定要去參觀的故宮博物院，請見以下英文影片（中文字幕），研究一下其中片段，記住一兩個故事，可以增加你帶他們去參觀時的談話樂趣：

- 國家地理頻道：透視內幕 - 國立故宮博物院 (1) –(3) https://www.YouTube.com/watch?v=KAQRm6x4Daw

跟台灣的歷史人文有關的紀念館與名人故居，大都有簡介影片與錄音導覽服務，但若需要英文導覽人員服務，通常要早點申請，你自己當然要先知道這些人、這些故事，才能充滿熱情地跟別人說為什麼值得去參觀，例如北部地區的：

- 國立台灣博物館National Taiwan Museum http://www2.ntm.gov.tw/index.htm

- 板橋的林本源園邸（即林家花園，The Ling Family Mansion and Garden）http://www.linfamily.ntpc.gov.tw/

- 士林官邸（The Shilin Presidential Residence）https://www.culture.gov.taipei/frontsite/shilin/index.jsp

以下適合學者型的訪客：
- 張大千紀念館（Chang, Da-Ch'ien Residence）http://www.npm.gov.tw/exh96/dai-chien/ch01.html

- 錢穆紀念館（The Ch'ieh Mu House）http://web.utaipei.edu.tw/~chienmu/

- 林語堂紀念館（The Lin Yutang House）http://www.linyutang.org.tw/big5/rest.asp

- 殷海光故居（Liberalism Yin Hai-Kuang Residence）http://www.yin.org.tw/about_residence.html

Activity 3 Understanding and applying words, idioms, and phrases

Useful expressions	Chinese meaning
1. annual meeting	年會
2. For once in my life, ...	一生一次
3. Ever since	自從
4. make a difference	有影響、有關係
5. I can't agree more.	非常同意
6. A bunch of us	一夥人
7. Even though...	縱使、即使
8. I would love to.	我非常樂意
9. make room for	讓出空位
10. spicy beef noodles	麻辣牛肉麵
11. head out	出去
12. freshen up	打扮、梳洗變得煥然一新

Unit 5-2 Enjoying the Night Market 夜市，這是一定要的

嘉莉：哇！多麼不可思議的夜市！

比爾：非常令人驚訝不是嗎？這夜市每晚這個時候總是特別熱鬧。

嘉莉：所以我們要怎麼進攻這個夜市怪物？我可沒多少信心嚐試古怪食物喔。

比爾：哈哈…不用擔心。我可以帶你遠遠離開那些古怪食物，像臭豆腐。

嘉莉：不要！我還是想嚐一下。但你得幫我吃我吃不下的食物。

比爾：沒問題，太容易了！

（片刻後）

比爾：喂，臭豆腐一客！

嘉莉：我的天啊…好難聞的味道啊。我正設法說服自己說：這東西吃起來應該比聞起來好一點。

比爾：如果你把它當作是起司，可能會覺得比較舒服。它跟起司一樣都是發酵食物。

嘉莉：好主意。把它想像成「油炸起司」！我要吃了喔。（喀嗤！喀嗤！）

比爾：所以呢？…你覺得怎麼樣啊？

嘉莉：你的建議真的有用ㄟ！我剛才自己嚇自己，以為它會是黏糊糊的。其實還不錯。那脆脆的感覺…還有泡菜，把油膩感降低了不少。

比爾：聽你這麼說我就放心了。那我們再去吃烤雞屁股如何？

嘉莉：迫不及待！開玩笑的啦。

比爾：沒關係的。那麼來點煎餃。

嘉莉：比爾，煎餃裡面是什麼餡料？

比爾：等我一下啦。

Activity 1 Listening practice

請把你聽到的字圈起來。

1. night market
2. at night
3. monster
4. funky
5. finish the rest
6. That's easy for me.
7. Here you go.
8. smells
9. cheese
10. Good idea.
11. What do you think?
12. are good combination
13. butts

14. kidding

15. fried dumplings

16. Wait up.

Activity 2 Disussion

1. 除了臭豆腐，夜市裡還有什麼外國人會覺得奇怪的食物？

2. 為什麼臭豆腐跟起士很像？像在哪裡？

3. 除了食物，夜市裡還可以看到什麼東西？

Activity 3 Understanding and applying words, idioms, and phrases

Part 1

下面的說法，是從剛才的對話抽出來的。首先請了解意義。接著開口說出聲，讓自己熟練。然後跟同學表演兩三分鐘的小短劇，請盡量套用以下的句子。

1. How do we attack this monster? 現在怎麼進攻這個夜市怪物？

2. I am trying to convince myself that...(finish this sentence with your own words.) 我設法說服自己說…

3. Your suggestion really worked! 你的建議真的有用！

4. I'm relieved to hear that. 聽你這樣說我就放心了！

5. Can't wait! 等不及了！

6. Just kidding. 開玩笑的啦！

Part 2

熟悉下列的語詞：

1. attack this monster 攻擊怪物（此處怪物為「夜市」，可能因為它很大佔地很廣。）

2. funky items 古怪的東西

3. fermented food products 發酵的食品

4. psych myself out 自己這麼想著
5. slimy and gooey 黏黏的
6. crunchiness 脆度

深入學習參考資料

台灣十大夜市
1. Taiwan Flowers Night Market 花園夜市（台南）
2. Feng Chia Night Market 逢甲夜市（台中）
3. Shilin Night Market 士林夜市（臺北）
4. Luodon Night Market 羅東夜市（羅東）
5. Liouhe Tourist Night Market 六合夜市（高雄）
6. Keelung Miaokou Night Market 基隆廟口夜市
7. Raohe St. Night Market 饒河街夜市（臺北）
8. Tonghua Night Market 通化夜市（臺北，臨江街夜市）
9. Huaxi St. Night Market 華西街夜市（臺北萬華）
10.Rueifong Night Market 瑞豐夜市（高雄）

台灣夜市食物
1. Pearl Milk Tea 珍珠奶茶
   Bubble tea 泡沫紅茶
   Tapioca tea 珍珠奶茶（在美國的說法）
   Boba tea 波霸奶茶（在美國的說法，直接以中文發音）
2. Oyster Omelet 蚵仔煎
3. Stinky Tofu 臭豆腐
4. Deep-fried Chicken Cutlets 炸雞排
5. Braised Pork On Rice 滷肉飯
6. Luwei/Soy Sauce Braise 滷味
7. Fried Cuttlefish Soup 生炒花枝羹
8. Xiao Long Tang Bao 小籠湯包
9. Scallion Pancake 蔥油餅

10.Shaved Ice 刨冰

11.Gua Bao 割包

12.Pork Chops in Chinese Medicine Soup 排骨十全大補

13.Oyster Vermicelli 蚵仔麵線

14.Taiwanese Meatballs 肉圓

15.Tea Egg 茶葉蛋

註1： 有人主張不要翻譯這些名稱，直接告訴訪客中文發音就好，如小籠湯包就是Xiao Long Tang Bao，不要翻作dumpling。的確，一翻譯味道好像就少了好多。這就好像生魚片全世界都知道它就叫sashimi，不需要翻作Raw Fish Piece一樣，因為意義真的大啊。（關於這一點，請進一步參考Unit 6-3。）

註2： 一面逛夜市，當然也要聊聊天。除了食物之外，關於夜市的話題，可以聊聊夜市形成的原因，夜市帶來的商機與工作機會，夜市當然也帶來不少問題，參考資訊請見：「生活趨勢：台灣夜市現象觀察」（by 奇想電子報，2012/09/21）

註3： 「台北旅遊網」提供了「百大小吃雙語菜單」提供包括蚵嗲（oyster vermicelli）等的中英文對照，還附上小吃照片，可自行下載使用。（http://new.travel.taipei/zh-tw/shop/100-night-market-snacks）

Chapter Six: Getting to Know More About You 介紹你自己

Unit 6-1 Chatting About Your Family 聊聊你的家人

本文翻譯

（在演奏廳）

丹尼斯：葛林教授，剛剛宣布10分鐘後演奏要開始，我們應該關掉我們的手機。

葛林教授：哦，是的。我差一點忘了。讓我轉成靜音。…再多說些有關你家人的事吧，丹尼斯。你家人住在台北嗎？

丹尼斯：事實上，我祖父母，我父母和我都住在一起。哦，還有我們的狗酷奇。

葛林教授：真的？這是一般的居住安排狀況嗎？

丹尼斯：現在這種情況在臺北比較少，但是仍然可以看到三代同堂住在同一屋簷下。有時甚至是四代同堂。

葛林教授：真是令人驚訝！你喜歡嗎？

丹尼斯：你可能會覺得很驚訝，但是我真的喜歡。我父母親和祖父母喜歡我在他們身邊，我也覺得他們好疼我。他們常開玩笑地指責我，說我就愛留在他們身邊，根本是因為想吃免錢的飯菜，還有人免費打掃。我還滿同意他們的說法的。嘻嘻…。

葛林教授：從你的描述，我可以想像這是個美滿的家庭。但你有想過要搬出去嗎？

丹尼斯：並沒有。他們真的很尊重屬於我的空間，這就是為什麼我們感情很好。我們住在新裝修過的兩層樓房，所以空間很夠。我也不見得常常有機會睏在他們身邊。

葛林教授：這是一個很有趣的觀點。你很幸運。

丹尼斯：是啊，我非常幸運。哦，指揮來了。

葛林教授：我很興奮能來看這演奏會。謝謝邀請我來。

Activity 1 Listening practice

聽CD並將正確的次序填入答案格中。

答案 1. __D__ 2. __C__ 3. __K__ 4. __H__ 5. __A__ 6. __I__

7. __G__ 8. __B__ 9. __F__ 10. __J__ 11. __E__

Activity 2 Discussion

1. 你住在哪類型的屋子？公寓或者透天屋？
2. 描述一下住的地方（如幾層樓，幾個房間等？）
3. 你跟誰一起住？你喜歡獨居或同居？為什麼？

Activity 3 Understanding and applying words, idioms, and phrases

Part 1

試著了解字詞的變化。然後兩人一組練習下列有用的詞語直到熟悉為止。

1. a house with two stories → a two-story house 一間兩層樓的房子。
2. remodel(v.) a condo → a remodeled(pp.-->adj.) condo → a remodeled two-story condo 一間重新整修過的兩層樓房

例：My family lives in a remodeled two-story condo. 我們家住在一間重新整修過的兩層樓房。

Part 2

請用以下的用語創造一個對話：

- Turn off our cell phones. 關掉手機。
- Put my phone on mute. 把手機設為靜音模式。
- How do you like it? 你喜歡嗎？
- accuse me of only staying around for... 指責我說我只為了…才留在這裡
- I can't agree more. 我非常同意。
- Did you every think about moving out? 你有沒有想過要搬出去住？
- a remodeled two-story condo 一間重新整修過的兩層樓房

- Here comes the conductor. 指揮來了。
1. 老師或者某一位同學先念出幾句帶有上述的詞語中文翻譯。
2. 大家舉手搶答說出英文句子。
3. 聲音夠大，句子又答對得一分。
4. 活動過後，每組試著創造一個對話，優勝隊得3分。
5. 得分最多的組得勝。

深入學習參考資料

房子的種類：

- 都會區比較多公寓華廈apartment，租來的就加rented，買下來有產權的是condo（condominium的簡稱）。
  句型：My family lives in a condominium apartment 或 a rented apartment.
- 透天房舍，若是一整排連在一起的稱作townhouse.
  句型：My family lives in a three-story townhouse.（在美國住townhouse每個月一般都要繳交兩三百美金的社區管理費 the maintenance fee）。
- 獨棟房舍，就是house.
- 小套房I live in a small studio (apartment).（與旅店裡的套房suite概念不同。）
- 若是跟人分租：I share an apartment with three girls/a family.
- 學校宿舍 I live in a dormitory on campus. My dorm room is small but nice and cozy（溫馨舒適）。
- 坪數 ping：
  「坪」不是歐美熟悉的概念，只有在日本或曾被日本統治過的地方，如台灣，才會用。所以必須換算成平方英尺（美國用）或平方公尺（其他國家用），他們才會有概念。
  一坪約 = 36 平方英呎（36 square feet 美）
  　　　= 3.305125 平方公尺（3.3 square meters 歐洲&其他國家）。
  例句：Our home is about 1368 square feet or 125 square meters.
  　　　我們家大概有38坪：

例句：The condo apartments in my neighborhood cost more than 500,000 NT dollars（five hundred thousand NT dollars）per ping now.

我們家那個區段，一坪買起來不只50萬台幣。

- 聊聊房子的社會話題：

Some people made a good living by <u>flipping properties</u>. They may remodel an old house and flip it for a quick profit, forcing the government <u>to cool off the housing market</u> by raising taxes.

有些人靠高價轉賣房地產獲利。他們可能裝修一下舊屋，就轉手獲利。逼著政府不得不提高稅率以打壓房市。

Unit 6-2 Chatting About Your Favorites
聊聊你最愛的消遣活動

本文翻譯

葛蘭特：嘿，雷，在展示攤位值班久了，出去休息一下如何？人潮已退，我想可以由助手接手招呼客人。

雷：好主意！我們去呼吸新鮮空氣吧！

（在展示中心外面）

葛蘭特：所以，告訴我，你在辦公室那麼忙，辦公室以外的時間喜歡做什麼？

雷：沒什麼興奮、刺激的，我喜歡每周到本地運動中心幾次。

葛蘭特：這樣噢？你在那兒做些什麼？

雷：嗯，運動中心是市政府經營的，價格很便宜。我通常去游泳，但是天氣好時，我也會在跑道上慢跑。

葛蘭特：運動是保持白天精力的一個好方法。我也會盡量常常運動。

雷：我太太有時會跟我去，但要看她的時間而定。我們喜歡做的就是晚餐後散步。散步讓我們可以追上進度（知道彼此生活中發生的新鮮事）。

葛蘭特：嗯，真羅曼蒂克，雷。我不知道你有這一面。周末你通常做什麼？

雷：差不多吧，我想想⋯，我們周末通常有很多雜事，比方處理日常瑣事啦，或者和家人朋友聊天。最近我們和朋友開始健行。

葛蘭特：我想我看過你臉書上的相片。有些小徑非常令人驚艷。

雷：假如你喜歡，歡迎加入我們。

葛蘭特：聽起來好有趣。下次我再來台灣，就要尾隨你們。哦，我們最好在助手緊張到不知所措前，趕快回去攤位吧。

雷：對。我們回去吧。

Activity 1 Listening practice

圈起聽到的字（劃線的是答案）。

Grant: Hey Ray, how about taking a (bread / <u>break</u>) from booth duty? The trade show crowd is (<u>dying</u> / trying) down so I think the assistants can (candle / <u>handle</u>) the visitors by themselves.

Ray: That's a good idea. Let's get some fresh air.

(*Outside the convention center*)

Grant: So, tell me, with your busy work life, what do you like to do (<u>outside</u> / inside) the office?

Ray: It's nothing (interesting / <u>exciting</u>), but I'd like to go to the local sports center a few times a week.

Grant: Oh yeah? What do you do there?

Ray: Yeah. The sports center is run by the city and it's pretty (<u>inexpensive</u> / expensive). I usually swim but if the weather is nice, I'll (<u>jog</u> / walk) around the track.

Grant: Exercising is a great way to keep up the energy level in the daytime. I also try to work out as (<u>often</u> / usually) as I can.

Ray: My wife joins me sometimes, but it depends on her (plan / <u>schedule</u>). Our favorite thing to do is to go for a walk after dinner. It gives us some time to (<u>catch</u> / get) up with each other.

Grant: That's kind of romantic, Ray. I didn't know this side pf you.
What do you usually do on (weekdays / the <u>weekend</u>)?

Ray: More of the same. Just kidding. Let's see... our weekends are usually filled with a little bit of everything like doing chores around the house and (<u>hanging</u> / taking) out with family or friends. (<u>Recently</u> / Secretly), we and some friends have started hiking.

Grant: I think I've seen pictures that you posted on Facebook. Some of those trails are (surprising / <u>stunning</u>).

Ray: If you like, you're welcome to join us.

Grant: That sounds like fun. I'll be sure to (<u>tag</u> / bag) along when I return to Taiwan next time. Oh, we better get back before the assistants start getting nervous.

Ray: You're right. Let's (hand / <u>head</u>) back.

Activity 2 Discussion

1. 你周末都做些什麼事？出去還是在家？
2. 您曾經去過運動中心嗎？請描述附近的一家運動中心，他們有什麼設施？你都做些什麼（活動）？
3. 描述一項你常做的或很喜歡的運動。跟你的朋友以英文討論，假想好像在跟國外訪客討論一樣。

Activity 3 Understanding and applying words, idioms, and phrases

Part 1
試著找同學唸出下面的句子，並想想看它們會被用在那些場合吧！

Part 2
瞭解片語跟句子的意思後，試著把左邊跟右邊的句子做配對再連起來。接著，全班分成四組進行比賽。老師會唸出左邊句組中的其中一句，學生聽到後搶答，最快舉手的那一組必須說出右邊句組中配對的句子，並在搶答結束後，上台演出1-3分鐘包含左右兩個配對句子的小短劇。搶答成功並回答出正確右邊句子得一分，順利演出小短劇得三分。得最多分的那一組獲得勝利喔！

深入學習參考資料

在台灣一般大眾喜歡的運動有biking（騎單車）、hiking（健行）、jogging（慢跑）、dancing（跳舞）、yoga（瑜珈）、gigong（氣功）、taking a day trip（一日遊）等。一大清早公園內、校園內都可看到跳舞、瑜珈、氣功等的身影。另外，社交舞（social dance）、熱舞（pop dance）、扇子舞（fan dance）、排舞（line dance）也很普遍。

可以這樣說：Activities that Taiwanese enjoy include biking, hiking, jogging, and many others that you can think of. Of course, gigone and more traditional Chinese exercises are also popular, but mostly among senior citizens. You can see them in parks or school campuses doing these exercises early in the morning.

這幾年來北市、新北市、台中等都開始提供另類交通工具與休閒運動Youbike（台北）、iBike（台中）、C-Bike（高雄）。其他景點區也都有私人租借的各種腳踏車。騎腳踏車成為人們最夯的交通工具與休閒活動。

可以這樣說：Biking is particularly easy in big cities both as a form of transportation and a leisure activity. There are rental stations all over the city for Youbikes in Taipei, iBikes in Taichung, and C-Bikes in Kaohsiung.

每個城市收費不同。以下為台北市YouBike104年的費率：

會員使用費率為：

每次騎乘前30分鐘付費5元（自104年1月1日起實施）。

騎乘逾30分鐘，但於4小時內還車，費率為每30分鐘10元。

騎乘逾4小時，但於8小時內還車，第4~8小時費率為每30分鐘20元。

騎乘逾8小時，於第8小時起將以每30分鐘40元計價。

單次租車的收費為：

騎乘4小時內,費率為每30分鐘10元。

騎乘逾4小時,但於8小時內還車,第4~8小時費率為每30分鐘20元。

可以這樣說:

Every city charges for their public bicycles differently. For example, in Taipei, with a YouBike membership, you pay five NT dollars for the first 30 minutes. Between 30 minutes to the fourth hour, it's 10 NT dollars for every 30 minutes. Between the fourth and the eighth hour, it's 20 NT dollars for every 30 minutes. After the eighth hour, you need to pay 40 NT dollars for every 30 minutes. Without membership, it's a bit expensive -- 10 NT dollars for the first 30 minutes, and 20 NT dollars for every 30 minutes between the fourth and eighth hour.

- Information for Youbike: http://taipei.youbike.com.tw/en/index.php

- Steps for renting a Youbike: http://taipei.youbike.com.tw/en/f42.php

Unit 6-3 **Dining at Home** 請他回家吃飯

本文翻譯

艾倫:凱倫,請坐。我媽媽說請你把這裡當作自己的家,可別客氣喔,吃得愈多,她愈開心!

凱倫:好貼心啊,艾倫!謝謝洪先生、洪太太。請跟你父母親說,這桌菜看起來好棒喔,我可要把我的禮貌往窗外扔了喔!

艾倫:太好了!整個學期我都好想念我家的家常菜。因為你來,我總算也可以好好享受媽媽的手藝了!

凱倫:希望這樣問不會失禮,你可以跟我說說看這是些什麼菜嗎?別擔心,我可是很有冒險精神的。

艾倫：哈哈，不好意思喔，這些都是常見的家庭料理，雖然如此，每位媽媽都有她的獨家口味。除了炒青菜外，我媽媽還準備了好吃的醬汁蒸排骨、番茄炒蛋，還有滷豆干。如果你想吃豬血糕或臭豆腐，我們得明天上夜市吃去。

凱倫：哇，我從來沒吃過這樣的菜色。這排骨是什麼口味啊？

艾倫：嗯，這有點像是排骨切成小塊，醃過蒜、薑和其他香料。但不是烤的或醃的，這道菜傳統上就是蒸的。醬汁比較稀，非常下飯！中國菜裡面，有很多炒的跟蒸的菜色。好廚師一定有各式各樣的手藝與拿手好菜。相信我，今晚的菜色在夜市裡可是找不到的。

凱倫：等不及了！

艾倫：正好，我媽媽也叫我別說話了！

洪媽媽說：開動！（並作手勢叫大家開動）

凱倫：我還真喜歡開動這兩個字的聲音。

Activity 1 Listening practice

接著，就是你得自己努力的時候囉，當你熟練到想都不用想就會說出口，就是你的了！

建議練習方式：

- 找個好朋友一起練習，兩人角色扮演，這樣做練習比較不孤單。
- 自己也可以同時扮演兩個角色，這就不怕說得不好，也不會害羞了。
- 還可以錄音一個角色，然候真人的自己再扮演另一角（說話的速度要跟上喔）。
- 當然你還可以自行發明其他方法。總而言之， 讓自己一面練習、一面覺得好玩是很重要的。

Activity 2 Discussion

再仔細看看Aaron（艾倫）如何解釋他母親的拿手菜：

大部分的菜色，除非對方吃過看過，不然就算你用中文都沒辦法藉著一個簡單的詞彙就讓別人了解。比方說過年吃的「佛跳牆」，光給個中文名詞，不知道的人一定還是一頭霧水，更何況是給英文名詞？這時候你需要用烹調方法、食材、食品的外觀形態、口感、甚至歷史故事、文化風俗加以形容與說明。這就有得聊了，對不？

你們家也有獨家美味嗎？學校附近有什麼特別有人氣的食物嗎？請試試看用下面表格內的英文，相互搭配著，形容一樣美食給同學猜猜看。記得喔，不要硬作字面上的翻譯，要像Aaron一樣，多給些資訊，讓別人具體了解。

Cooking technique 烹調方法	Ingredient 食材	Shape 食品的外觀	Taste 口感
少油慢煎的 sauté, fried 油炸的deep fried 炒的stir fried （炒蛋 scrambled egg）	蔬菜類vegetables： 蘆筍asparagus 筍bamboo shoot 豆芽bean sprouts 青彩椒bell peppers 苦瓜bitter melons 高麗菜cabbage 芹菜celery 白菜Chinese cabbage 蒜garlic，薑ginger 青蔥green onion 蘿蔔radish 西生菜lettuce 茄子egg plants 菇mushroom 香菜parsley 芋頭taro 薯類（山藥等）yam 地瓜、甘薯sweet potato	刨成絲的shredded 切成塊的 cut into small pieces 捲roll（春捲、潤餅 steamed spring roll： 燒餅clay oven roll 或the flaky sesame pastry） 棒stick（油條fried bread stick或 Chinese donut） 炭烤串燒grilled kebab	酸的sour 甜的sweet 苦的bitter 辣的spicy 鹹的salty

Cooking technique 烹調方法	Ingredient 食材	Shape 食品的外觀	Taste 口感
水煮的 boiled	黃豆soy bean 醬油soy source 豆腐tofu 豆干bean curds 臭豆腐stinky tofu 豆花tofu pudding	水餃dumplings	口感滑潤 smooth
燉煮的 stewed	海帶、海苔seaweed	饅頭buns	怪怪的funky
滷的 braised	海產Seafood： 透抽squid 小蝦shrimp 大蝦pawn 蟹crab 蛤蠣clams 蚵oysters 鰻魚eel 鮑魚abalone 章魚octopus	餛飩wonton	脆脆QQ的 crunchy
蒸的steamed		粥porridge, congee	湯濃濃的 creamy， rich，thick 咖啡的濃是 strong

Cooking technique 烹調方法	Ingredient 食材	Shape 食品的外觀	Taste 口感
火爐烤的grilled or roasted 焗烤的baked 鐵板 iron-platter or pan-fried	家禽類poultry： 雞chicken 鴨duck 腿leg 翅膀wing	飯rice 糯米sticky rice（或 glutinous rice） 糙米husked rice	很重的醬油味 It has a strong soy sauce taste.
煙燻的smoked 風乾的dried	豬肉pork 排骨rib 絞肉ground port 香腸sausage 豬血糕blood pudding, pig 腰子liver 大腸 intestine 屁股butt	麵noodles 冬粉green bean noodles 米粉rice noodle	油膩greasy 清淡light 太淡了too plain，（或 thin，light， 皆可，但plain 還有平平、乏 善可陳的感 覺）
發酵過的 fermented	牛肉beef 牛肉乾beef jerky	糰、丸子ball	有起士的感覺 cheesy
泡菜的pickled 醃過醬汁的 marinated	水果類fruits： 芭樂guava 楊桃star fruit 芒果mango 釋迦custard apple or sakya 蓮霧 bell fruit	三明治sandwich 例如：棺材板 deep-fried sandwich	黏糊糊的 slimy and gooey 質地很有趣 It has an interesting texture. （有暗示不太 喜歡的意思）

Cooking technique 烹調方法	Ingredient 食材	Shape 食品的外觀	Taste 口感
糖醋的 sweet & sour 酸辣的 hot & sour 麻辣的 hot & spicy	中式甜品 desserts： 紅豆red bean，bean 豆沙bean paste 綠豆mung bean（綠豆 若說成green bean就成 了豌豆）	糕餅cake，patty （也可以用在酥， 例如鳳梨酥是 Pineapple Cake）	像在吃中藥 It tastes like Chinese medicine.
	薏仁pearl barley（是去 殼的大麥barley 不去殼的薏仁叫semen coicis） 麥角oatmeal 芋頭taro 蓮子lily seeds		
咖哩的curried	牛軋糖nougat 豆花tofu pudding 仙草grass jelly 愛玉Vegetarian gelatin	湯soup 火鍋hot pot	醬汁較多 The gravy is on the watery side.
有勾芡的with cornstarch	蛋egg 皮蛋thousand-year-old eggs 炒蛋scrambled egg 蚵仔煎oyster omelet	細粉powder 花生粉 peanut powder	下飯很棒 It is so good over rice.

*註：因為可以列出的東西太多了，沒辦法全包，本表盡量選擇台灣人常會 用到的字。

Activity 3 Understanding and applying words, idioms, and phrases

Example 1:

Dad: Hey, all you have in your cupboard is pasta and tinned tomatoes.

Mom:　Yeh, I know, I haven't had chance to go shopping. Pasta is just my <u>go-to meal</u>.

Example 2:

Johnny:　Do you know what kind of glue I should use to stick two pieces of wood together?

Kevin:　I dunno. I'd jus tuse ABC. It's my <u>go-to glue</u>.

<u>吃素的說法</u>：I don't eat meat. 或 I am a vegetarian. 而生機飲食則稱作 organic food；精力湯 energy drink。很多人說自己是 a vegan，指的可能是一律不吃不用動物製品。西方人嘴上說不吃肉、吃素，但也有可能吃海鮮喔，跟我們熟悉的素食習慣與文化不同，大家還是要細問。體貼周到的你最好都問：Is there anything you do not eat?

<u>interesting 是個很有意思的字</u>。有時候老外說 It is interesting，其實是有不喜歡的意思，這時你可以補上一句：You mean you don't like it? 讓他解釋一下。

<u>叫人家爸媽 Mr. and Mrs. Hong?</u> 講究禮節的我們台灣人總會叫朋友的父母親為叔叔阿姨、伯父伯母（至少連續劇是這麼演的），但英文不會這麼把別人看做一家親，所以Karen 叫 Mr. and Mrs. Hong 就已經是對長輩非常有禮貌了，一般就是叫名字而已。同理，你若是有小孩，就不必讓他們叫外國朋友叔叔阿姨，這樣可能會讓人不舒服喔。那怎辦呢？叫名字就好囉，並不失禮的。講究一點的話就用這樣的說法：Mr. and Mrs. + 姓氏，如 Mr. and Mrs. Hong.

以英文教做台式料理的書：

台灣書店裡中英對照的食譜已經不容易找到了，完全寫給外籍人士的、以他們的角度寫的更少。前次小編帶外籍友人逛誠品書店（Eslite

Bookstore），但想找一本以英文書寫的台式食譜（Taiwanese recipes）都找不到，友人好失望。（反而是在英美當地可能比較有機會找得到喔！）以下是最近發現的一本在台灣網路書店可以買到的台式食譜，還請各位烹調高手參考並加油：

Erway, Cathy/ Lee, Peter (PHT) (2015). The Food of Taiwan: Recipes from the Beautiful Island. Houghton Mifflin Harcourt.

Chapter Seven: Sharing Our Cultures
分享自己的文化

Unit 7-1 Taking up Native Dialects 閒聊家庭語言背景

前言：本章是關於家族語言的問題，是屬於比較有深度的文化討論。很多外籍訪客對文化非常有興趣，你一定要能夠談一點自己的文化，才能與他們交流。

本文翻譯

奈特麗：你的中文進步到讓我印象深刻。

凱　倫：謝謝！我是說「Xie Xie」！在這裡待久了真的讓我學比較多中文。雖然學了點中文，但是還沒有機會學台語。

比　爾：事實上，不是只有你一個人如此，有多少的年輕人也不會說父母親或祖父母的方言。他們可能聽得懂，但是說會有困難。

凱　倫：真的？

奈特麗：真的。舉例來說，我爸爸的父母親來自廣東省，當地的人主要說廣東話。我媽媽的家庭已經住在台灣好幾代了，他們說台灣話。自然而然，我父母親都會很流利的說上一輩子的方言，但是我不會。

凱　倫：這太糟了。這些方言說得不多嗎？

比　爾：對我來說，我聽得懂客家話，但是我無法真正的將我的想法轉為客語。這就是現況。國語是學校中所教和所說的主要語言，小孩子回家後就不習慣說他們的母語。因為疏於練習，說的能力就流失了。

奈特麗：我同意比爾的說法。我們的方言被學校課程忽略了很久。我們有來自中國各處非常豐富的不同民族文化的人。但是因為我們過去文化和政治的複雜，我們這一代愈來愈少人會用這些美麗的語言溝通。

比　爾：當然我們也不能怪罪國家或學校。這樣太簡化議題了。我們在家裡所做的也是重要的學習。

凱　倫：我了解你的意思。我媽媽來自俄羅斯，但是我只能聽得懂俄語。
　　　　當我想講簡單的句子時，我舌頭就打結了。

比　爾：我比較不會（為自己的不會說）覺得尷尬。嚴肅一點地講，我滿
　　　　高興我們的學校現在投入較多的資源，教小孩子區域語言和本土
　　　　文化，電視上也有教育性節目設法達成這個使命。

凱　倫：很高興聽到啊。我想小小的改變可以從我們自己開始。嘿，我知
　　　　道了！你們兩位今天教我國語以外的方言如何？

奈特麗和比爾：聽起來很有趣！

註：本對話內容中"We have such a diverse mix of people <u>from</u> all over
　　China and incredibly rich indigenous cultures."之<u>from</u>只有一個，但
　　Listening Practice Part2有兩個form，兩者都可以接受，雖然口氣上略
　　有不同。

Activity 1 Listening practice

Part 1

Listen to the CD and choose the correct answers.

39

In Taiwan, many young people are unable to speak the dialect of their
parents and grandparents. They may understand it, but they have a hard time
speaking it. For instance, my father's parents are from Canton Province
where people mainly speak Cantonese. My mother's family are from
Shanghai where people speak Shanghai dialect. Naturally, my parents are
fluent in the dialects of their elders, but I am not. Because I was born in
Taiwan, my Taiwanese is better than my Cantonese and Shanghai dialect.

答案 1.　　B　　2.　　D　　3.　　C

Part 2

Listen to the CD and circle the correct the answers.

40

Our dialects have been ignored by our school <u>curriculum</u> for a long time. We have such a <u>diverse</u> mix of people from all over China and from incredibly rich indigenous cultures. However, <u>because of</u> the cultural and political complexities of our past, fewer and fewer people in our <u>generation</u> are able to communicate in those beautiful words. Of course, we can't just <u>blame</u> the government or schools. That would be simplifying the issue. What we do at home is also an important <u>element</u> of learning too.

Now, I'm glad that our schools are dedicating more resources in teaching kids regional dialects and <u>native</u> cultures. There are also educational programs on TV <u>with</u> this mission too. Little by little, our dialects can be kept.

 1. __curriculum__ 2. __diverse__ 3. __because of__

4. __generation__ 5. __blame__ 6. __element__

7. __native__ 8. __with__

Activity 2 Discussion

1. Language和dialect這兩字有什麼不同？

   Mandarin是我們目前所謂的「國語」或「漢語」的意思，也就是說「華語、普通話」。解釋為「官場使用的語言」出自明朝時，葡萄牙人對大明官員的稱呼。據說滿清帝國有「國語」和「官話」之分，「國語」＝滿洲語，「官話」是說承襲明朝官場使用之語言。所以Mandarin只是發音趨近「滿大人」，充其量僅語言內容受到滿洲語影響，基本上跟滿洲語無關。

   目前台灣的主要方言與比率：

   Taiwanese Hokkien 70%

Formosan languages of aboriginal tribes 2%

Mandarin Chinese 12%

其他方言的英文說法：

Cantonese 廣東話

Shanghai dialect 上海話

Hakka 客家話

Sichuan dialect 四川話

Hunanese 湘話 / 湖南話

Gan 贛話 / 江西話

Northern Min 閩北話

Southern Min 閩南話

Eastern Min 閩東話

Central Min 閩中話

2. 除了中文，你還會說其他的方言嗎？假如會的話請說幾句讓你的同學聽聽？

3. 你會說你祖父母的方言嗎？為什麼？（請說明原因。）

Activity 3 Understanding and applying words, idioms and phrases

Part 1

Useful expressions

練習下列的詞語。需要時也可用手機查用法。

- pick up (more) Chinese 隨時學

  It's easy to pick up English in the big cities in Taiwan.

- put my thought into words 將思想轉換為語言

  Having learned English for 10 years, it's easy to put my thought into English.

- agree with 同意

  Chris is a know-it-all. I often find it hard to agree with him on most of his suggestions.

- diverse 多種多樣的

  My brother Owen is awesome. He has diverse interests, such as, music, sports, and traveling.
- indigenous 本土的

  Koalas are indigenous to Australia.
- simplify 簡單化

  Whenever you teach beginners English, you should simplify your sentences.
- element 元素

  Honesty, punctuality, and devotion are elements of a good student.
- get tongue tied 舌頭打結

  Whenever talking about language, Mary gets tongue tied because she doesn't have the language gene.
- regional 地區性的

  Water rationing is regional, not island-wide.

Part 2

The following two patterns are commonly used. Be sure to know how to use them. 請注意以下兩個常見的字與出現的位置。

1. With ...,
   - **With** a lot of books in my arms, I can't hold a strap on the bus.
     手上抱著一堆書，我就不能抓著車上的拉環。
   - **With** (drinking) a lot of beer, I was kind of tipsy walking on the street.
     喝了一些啤酒，我走在路上就搖搖晃晃的了。

2. Though 雖然：（請注意though出現的位置）
   - Being here for a longer period of time really helped me pick up more Chinese. I still have no luck learning Taiwanese, **though**.
     在此處待了一段比較長的時間真的讓我學到比較多中文，雖然我還是對學台語沒什麼運氣。

• Seriously, **though**, I'm glad that our schools are dedicating more resources in teaching kids regional dialects and native cultures.

說真的，雖然如此，我還滿高興學校現在為地方語言與文化投入較多的資源。

More practice再多一點點練習：

I love him. My parents don't like him though.

我愛他，雖然我父母不喜歡他。

這個句子，寫成以下的幾種形式，都是可接受的。

→ My parents don't like him though I love him.

→ Though I love him, my parents don't like him.

→ I love him, but my parents' don't like him.

Unit 7-2 Learning Some Chinese Expressions
教他幾句簡單華語

本文翻譯

（艾倫和凱倫、嘉麗在酒吧內）

嘉麗：這真是很酷的酒吧，艾倫。你來這酒吧多久了？

艾倫：我第二次來。當凱倫邀請我時，我馬上想到這個地方。

凱倫：選得好，我的朋友。在這熱熱的晚上這杯飲料讓我感到很清涼。
看，我幾乎快喝完了。

嘉麗：我們再叫一杯給凱倫。怎麼說（中文的）再來一杯？

艾倫：「再來一杯，謝謝」。字面上意思就是再來一杯，謝謝。

嘉麗：「再來一杯」。讓我試試看。我還沒學會這一句話之前，我都只用
眼睛看著服務人員，然後再指著我的杯子。

凱倫：好酷！好像是某個神秘的角色，在偵探小說中所做的事。

嘉麗：「謝謝」（所有的人都笑了）開玩笑的。我怎麼樣都不夠酷的。

凱倫：我覺得說「不好意思」這句話，在當我要問方向或想叫一位服務員
時，還滿好用的。

嘉麗：真的是很好的方法。就算你只知道幾個字，當你盡力說那個語言的
時候，對方就知道你真的在努力。

艾倫：而且能表現出尊敬和真誠的態度。這在台灣的文化來說很重要。

凱倫：知道了！以後都讓嘉麗幫我們點餐。你需要練習。

嘉麗：「等一下」，你這個提議我可不確定喔。

Activity 1 Listening practice

42

1-3題聽力測驗

Woman:　This is really a cool bar. How long have you been coming here?

Man:　　This is my third time. One of my friends brought me here once.
Then I was immediately attracted by its atmosphere.

Man: By the way, what do you like to drink?

Woman: What do you suggest since you have been here three times?

Man: I like espresso. But they told me latte and milk tea are good, too.

Woman: I'll drive whatever you order for me.

Man: (flagging down the waiter) Waiter, two espressos.

 1.　B　2.　C　3.　D

 43

4-11題聽力測驗

Karen: This drink is so (4) refreshing. Look, I have almost finished it!

Carrie: We'll need to order another one for Karen. How do you say one more?

Aaron: "Zai lai yi bei, xiexie", (5) which means one more glass, thank you.

Carrie: "Zai lai yi bei, xiexie". Let me try it now. Before I learned this phrase, I only (6) looked at the waiter and pointed to my glass.

Karen: "How cool!" Seems like what a mysterious character (7) would do in a detective novel.

Carrie: Xiexie. (All laughing) Just kidding. I'm anything but cool.

Karen: I think saying "bu hao yi si" goes a long way when I'm trying to get directions or (8) flagging down a waiter.

Carrie: That's a pretty good approach. Even if you know only a few words, you try your best to (9) speak up and really let the other person know that you're trying.

Aaron: And, it shows respect and sincerity. That's big in (10) Taiwanese culture.

Karen: I know! Let's make Carrie (11) order for us from now on. You need to practice.

Carrie: "Deng yi xia!" I'm not so sure about this proposal.

Activity 2 Discussion

你有沒有教外國朋友說中文的經驗？若有，請說說那樣的經驗。若沒有，當你有機會時，你最先會教哪些中文句子？

深入學習參考資料

要教他們中文，你自己要先學會漢語拼音喔。請見以下Chinese Digger 的〔學習漢語拼音〕資訊

各種學習工具：http://chinesedigger.blogspot.tw/2008/05/learn-hanyu-pinyin.html

用63個字學會漢語拼音：http://chihcherng.blogspot.tw/2009/06/63.html

Unit 7-3 Visiting a Temple 參觀寺廟

本文翻譯

（奈特麗與嘉麗搭捷運到達了龍山寺。）

奈特麗：到了，嘉麗。這就是龍山寺。

嘉　麗：這地方真漂亮！

奈特麗：真令人驚艷，不是嗎？

嘉　麗：真是宏偉！我可以感受到這座廟的歷史。

奈特麗：龍山寺是台灣很多古廟中的一座。好幾世代以來，它為人們帶來了和平感和希望。注意到那香煙裊裊嗎？

嘉　麗：怎麼會錯過？我一向喜歡燒香的神秘感。或許香的煙把我們的訊息傳給神明。

奈特麗：這種想法很棒。

嘉　麗：謝啦。等下會有派對嗎？我看到很多人將食物和飲料放在桌上。

奈特麗：沒有，那些是給神明的供品。我祖母說：「當你進貢時，神明會
　　　　很快樂，所以會保佑大家平安。」

嘉　麗：所以這是一種賄賂？

奈特麗：哈哈。我會這麼說。但是我想這是一種幫助人們減輕憂慮和恐懼
　　　　的方法。

嘉　麗：這樣說很合理。嘿，那些人在祭壇旁做什麼？

奈特麗：好問題！他們正在用占卜的器具「擲筊」。通常當人們在人生中
　　　　遇到難解決的問題時，他們會求神明幫助找答案。他們占卜器具
　　　　落地時，他們就接收到神明的回應。

嘉　麗：真酷。我可以試試看嗎？

奈特麗：當然。但是求神時要心誠。之後，我再告訴妳別的。

嘉　麗：太棒了！這是一個有趣的經驗。

奈特麗：妳知道龍山寺只是台灣幾千座廟宇中的一間而已。妳不可能每間
　　　　都去看，但是妳現在已經了解廟宇了。

嘉　麗：你說的極是。我很高興我們來到這裡。

Activity 1 Listening practice

Part 1

Listen to the CD and fill in the blanks.

45

Natalie: Let's take MRT Blue Line to Longshan Temple.

Carrie:　Which station should we get off?

Natalie: Longshan Temple station.

Carrie:　Great, it's good to remember.

(*getting off the train*)

Natalie: Look! This is Longshan Temple.

Carrie:　What a marvelous place!

Natalie: Pretty awesome, isn't it?

Carrie: It is so grand! I can really feel the history of this temple.

Natalie: Longshan Temple is one of the oldest <u>temples</u> in Taiwan. For generations, it brought a <u>sense</u> of peace and hope to the people. Notice the light smoke over there?

Carrie: How can I miss it? I always loved the mystique of <u>burning incense</u>. Maybe the smoke <u>sends</u> our messages to the gods.

Natalie: That's a really nice thought.

Carrie: Thanks.

答案 1.   Blue   2.   station   3.   remember   4.   marvelous

      5.   temples   6.   sense   7.   burning incense   8.   sends

Part 2

Listen to the CD and answer the questions.

46

Taiwan has more than 10000 temples and there are three main varieties of temples: Buddhist, Taoist and Confucius temples. The oldest temple in Taiwan is Tianhou Temple in Makung, in the Penhu Islands, and has been in existence for over 300 years.

In Taipei, Longshan is the oldest temple, located in Taipei's Wanhua District. It was built in 1738 by settlers from Fujian, China. It was a place of worship and a gathering place for the Chinese settlers.

答案 1.   B   2.   C   3.   A

Activity 2 Discussion

1. 你曾經用占卜的器具「擲筊」嗎？解釋一下原因。

深入學習

Chinese Temple culture：擲筊 Divination

https://www.YouTube.com/watch?v=9hC1d9K8eTY

《問對了！神明才會告訴你答案》神啊！我該怎樣才能找到

好工作？

https://www.YouTube.com/watch?v=h1dbRMCURLQ

建議把你看到的影片內容講給訪客聽，他們一定覺得很有趣。

2. 台灣有多少不同宗教？在台灣有少座廟宇？又麼佛教廟宇和道教廟宇各有多少？查一下網路去找出答案。

- 根據內政部（Ministry of the Interior）統計，台灣有27種不同宗教，最主要的有：佛教Buddhism（35%）、道教Taoism（33%）、一貫道Yi guan tao（2.6%）、基督教Christianity（包括基督新教Protestant與天主教Roman Catholic）（1.3%）。

- 全台寺廟有11,400多座，平均每縣近600座，台南縣高居冠軍，高出平均數近一倍，其次是高雄縣和屏東。道教廟宇約佔78.3%，而佛教廟宇約佔19.6%。

- 如果你的訪客對宗教有興趣，全台有許多知名廟宇可參觀，例如南

部地區的佛光山佛陀博物館Fo Kung Shan Buddha Memorial Center http://www.fgsbmc.org.tw/）；部分教堂也有導覽服務，例如臺北新生南路天主教聖家堂（Holy Family Church）。另外位於台東公東高中的公東教堂（The Chapel of Kung-Tung），建築極美，非常值得參觀。此外，還可以

考慮參觀位於永和的世界宗教博物館：http://www.mwr.org.tw/（Museum of World Religions）

Activity 3 Understanding and applying words, idioms and phrases

Part 1
試著了解下列的字詞。之後,和同伴一起造句,直到熟練為止。

Part 2
兩人一組,利用上面的生字造句,2分鐘內造最多句子的人是贏家。可利用碼錶或手機上碼錶的功能來計時。

Part 3
3-4人一組,寫下廟裡可能所看到的東西,並大聲念出。注意每個字發音的正確性。

參考答案

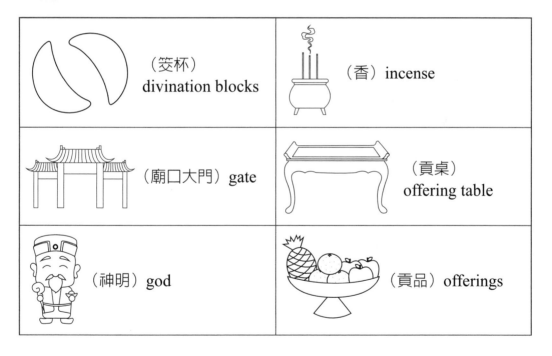

(筊杯) divination blocks	(香) incense
(廟口大門) gate	(貢桌) offering table
(神明) god	(貢品) offerings

（算命仙）fortune teller

（冥紙）
ghost money

（跪凳）kneeler

（香客）worshipper

附錄二：參考資料

A. 以下資料可以幫助大家設計旅遊行程，或提供資訊，全都可轉為英文版本：

- 觀光局 http://taiwan.net.tw/w1.aspx
- 台灣觀光巴士 http://www.taiwantourbus.com.tw/
- Free Half-day Tours http://eng.taiwan.net.tw/tour/index.htm
- 中正紀念堂兩廳院節目表 http://npac-ntch.org/en/

B. 相關書籍：（以出版年之近遠排列）

- 外國旅人遇到台灣驚豔。時報出版。李慕瑾／著，林芝安／採訪撰文（2015）
- 用英語遊Taipei：15經典台北旅遊景點（20K+1MP3）Discover Taipei in English: 15 Classic Tourist Destinations 寂天出版社，作者：Treva Adams, Hui-Hsien Chen (2014)
- 說英語Fun遊台灣（25K彩色+1MP3）Fun in Taiwan! The Best Guide to Taiwan
- 作者：Andrew Crosthwaite 譯者：林育珊，黃詩韻，蘇祥慧（2014）
- 台灣趴趴走Taiwan Follow Me!：EZ TALK總編嚴選特刊（1書1MP3）（2014）
- 輕鬆用英語介紹台灣（50K附MP3）作者：張文娟　出版社：雅典文化 （2013）
- OH! MY GUIDE! 臺灣超好玩。舒兆民、陳懷萱、黃琡華、林家盈，正中書局，出版日期：2013-08-30

- 認識台灣歷史1至10冊中文書，文魯彬／英文版編寫；吳密察／總策劃；劉素珍等／漫畫繪製；許豐明等／劇本編寫　耿柏瑞（Brian A. Kennedy）等，新自然主義，出版日期：2012-12-24
- 如何用英語介紹臺灣：讓你流暢將台灣文化等介紹給老外；使老外更了解台灣 = How to Introduce Taiwan in English／元叔編著（2012）
- 英文介紹台灣：實用觀光導遊英語〔彩圖三版〕（16K+1MP3）Taiwan in Simple English: The Best Guidebook for Travelers and Tour Guides作者：Paul O'Hagan、Peg Tinsley、Owain Mckimm／著，Zachary Fillingham、Cheryl Robbins／審訂譯者：蔡裴驊、郭菀玲、丁宥榆　出版社：寂天 (2012)
- Spotlight on Taiwan-Opening Taiwan to the World with CD/1片作者：Yolanda Chi · Isabel Chuo · Andy Hu · Susu Hung（文藻外語編著）出版社：東華（2009）
- 用英文遊台灣（附光碟）作者：黃玟君　出版社：聯經出版公司（2007）
- 瘋台灣系列DVD采昌國際多媒體
- FROM TEXT TO TALK：TAIWAN IN SIMPLE ENGLISH　作者：Paul O'Hagan 出版社：寂天（2006）

國家圖書館出版品預行編目資料

美語口語訓練／招靜琪，陳彥佑著.
－－初版. －－臺北市：五南，2016.07
　面；　公分
ISBN 978-957-11-8675-7（平裝）

1.英語　2.會話

805.188　　　　　　　　　105011135

1XOV

美語口語訓練

作　　者 — 招靜琪　陳彥佑

發 行 人 — 楊榮川

總 編 輯 — 王翠華

主　　編 — 朱曉蘋

封面設計 — 陳翰陞

校　　對 — 施雅婷

圖片來源 — IDJ圖庫

插　　圖 — 王郁涵　王姿婷

出 版 者 — 五南圖書出版股份有限公司

地　　址：106台北市大安區和平東路二段339號4樓

電　　話：(02)2705-5066　　傳　　真：(02)2706-6100

網　　址：http://www.wunan.com.tw

電子郵件：wunan@wunan.com.tw

劃撥帳號：01068953

戶　　名：五南圖書出版股份有限公司

法律顧問　林勝安律師事務所　林勝安律師

出版日期　2016年7月初版一刷

定　　價　新臺幣350元